P9-CCK-836

Dear Reader,

We're thrilled that some of Harlequin's most famous families are making an encore appearance! With this special Famous Families fifty-book collection, we are proud to offer you the chance to relive the drama, the glamour, the suspense and the romance of four of Harlequin's most beloved families—the Fortunes, the Bravos, the McCabes and the Cavanaughs.

Wedding bells are ringing for the infamous Bravos— even if they don't know it yet! The all-American clan created by *USA TODAY* bestselling author Christine Rimmer is the second family in our special collection. Its members are cowboys and billionaires, lawyers and private investigators. Their exploits take them from the mountains of Wyoming, to a small, close-knit town in California to the glitzy Vegas strip. But whether they're rich or down-to-earth, city or small-town bred, you'll fall in love with each of the Bravos as they take their own compelling journey to a happy ending.

And coming in May, you'll meet Dr. Jackson McCabe, as we introduce you to our next special family, the McCabes of Texas, by beloved author Cathy Gillen Thacker.

Happy reading,

The Editors

CHRISTINE RIMMER

came to her profession the long way around. Before settling down to write about the magic of romance, she'd been everything from an actress to a salesclerk to a waitress. Now that she's finally found work that suits her perfectly, she insists she never had a problem keeping a job—she was merely gaining "life experience" for her future as a novelist.

Christine is grateful not only for the joy she finds in writing, but for what waits when the day's work is through: a man she loves, who loves her right back, and the privilege of watching their children grow and change day to day. She lives with her family in Oregon. Visit Christine at www.christinerimmer.com.

FAMOUS FAMILIES

the BRAVOS

USA TODAY bestselling author

CHRISTINE RIMMER

The M.D. She Had to Marry

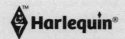

TORONTO NEW YORK LONDON
AMSTERDAM PARIS SYDNEY HAMBURG
STOCKHOLM ATHENS TOKYO MILAN MADRID
PRAGUE WARSAW BUDAPEST AUCKLAND

For Auralee Smith,
my mom, who's already had
one or two dedicated to her.
But such a terrific mom should get
grateful dedications on a regular basis.
I love you, Mom.
Here's to you…again.

Recycling programs
for this product may
not exist in your area.

ISBN-13: 978-0-373-36497-8

THE M.D. SHE HAD TO MARRY

www.Harlequin.com

Printed in U.S.A.

FAMOUS FAMILIES

The Fortunes

The Bravos by Christine Rimmer

The McCabes by Cathy Gillen Thacker

Dr. Cowboy
Wildcat Cowboy
A Cowboy's Woman
A Cowboy Kind of Daddy
A Night Worth Remembering
The Seven-Year Proposal
The Dad Next Door
The Last Virgin in Texas
Texas Vows: A McCabe Family Saga
The Ultimate Texas Bachelor
Santa's Texas Lullaby
A Texas Wedding Vow
Blame It on Texas
A Laramie, Texas Christmas
From Texas, With Love

The Cavanaughs by Marie Ferrarella

Racing Against Time
Crime and Passion
Internal Affair
Dangerous Games
The Strong Silent Type
Cavanaugh's Woman
In Broad Daylight
Alone in the Dark
Dangerous Disguise
The Woman Who Wasn't There
Cavanaugh Watch
Cavanaugh Heat

Chapter 1

On a sunny afternoon at the end of June, Lacey Bravo returned to the old homesteader's cabin behind the horse pasture at the Rising Sun Ranch to find Dr. Logan Severance waiting for her.

She had known he would come. Still, the sight of him, there in the shade of the rough-shingled overhang that served as the cabin's front porch, sent her pulse racing. Her palms on the steering wheel went clammy with sweat. She felt pulled in two directions at once. Her foolish heart urged her to rush into his arms. And something else, some contrary creature inside her, wanted only to spin her new SUV around and speed away, leaving nothing but a high trail of Wyoming dust in her wake.

Neither action was really an option. Throwing herself into his arms would only embarrass them both.

And as for running, well, Lacey had done plenty of that before she was even out of her teens. Eventually, she'd given it up. It never solved anything.

With a weary sigh, Lacey pushed the door open and maneuvered herself out from behind the wheel and down to the ground. She shut the door. Then, with as much dignity as she could muster, given that lately she tended to waddle like a duck, she plodded to the rear of the vehicle to get the two bags of groceries she had picked up in town.

She barely got the back door up before Logan was at her side. "I'll take those for you."

Her initial reaction was to object, to lift her chin high and announce haughtily, "I can carry my own groceries, thank you."

But she stifled the impulse. There would be dissension enough between them. There always had been. And now, with the baby coming, the opportunities for argument would no doubt be endless. Better to keep her mouth shut whenever possible.

His dark gaze swept over her. She wore a tentlike denim jumper, a pink T-shirt and blue canvas ballerina flats.

Ballerina. Hah. An image from an old Disney movie, of a hippo in ballet shoes and a tutu, flitted through her mind.

No, she was not at her best. And he looked great. Terrific. Fit and tanned, in khaki pants and a cream-colored polo shirt. He looked like a model on the cover of a Brooks Brothers catalog—and she looked like someone who'd eaten a beach ball for lunch. She knew she shouldn't let that bother her. But it did.

"Hasn't your doctor told you that at this point in your pregnancy, you shouldn't be driving?"

She gritted her teeth and granted him the tiniest of shrugs.

"Is that a 'yes'?"

Lacey exerted superhuman effort and did not roll her eyes. "Yes, Doctor. That is a 'yes.'"

He made a low, exasperated sound. "Then what are you doing behind the wheel of a car?"

"I treasure my independence."

The words may have sounded flippant, but Lacey did mean them. Doc Pruitt, who ran the clinic in the small nearby town of Medicine Creek, *had* been nagging her to avoid driving. And Tess, her cousin's wife, who lived in the main ranch house not a half a mile away, would have been glad to take Lacey wherever she needed to go. But to Lacey, a car—and the possession of the keys to it—meant self-determination. Never would she willingly give that up.

Except, perhaps, for the love of this man.

But not to worry. Her independence was safe. Logan's heart was otherwise engaged.

"Lacey," he said, in the thoroughly superior tone that had always made her want to throw something at him. "There are times in life when independence has to take a backseat to necessity. It's not good for you, or the baby, for you to—"

"Logan, can we at least get inside before you start telling me everything I'm doing wrong?"

He blinked. Maybe it actually occurred to him that he'd started criticizing her before he'd even bothered to say hello. Whatever. Without another word, he

scooped her grocery bags into his big arms and turned
toward the cabin. Lacey was left to shut the rear door
and trudge along in his wake, across the bare dirt yard,
past the dusty midnight-blue luxury car he had driven
there and up the two rickety steps to the cabin's front
entrance. On the porch, he stood aside for her to open
the door. Then she moved out of his way to let him go
first.

They entered the main living area, which was
small and dark and simply furnished. Lacey loved the
cabin—*had* loved it on sight. Though the light was
never good enough to paint by, the rough plank walls
pleased her artist's eye. And the layers of shadow were
interesting, dark and intense in the corners, fading out
to a pleasant dimness in the center of the room. Beyond
the main room, there was a small sleeping nook in the
northeast corner and a bathroom in a lean-to outside
the back door.

Logan didn't seem to share her admiration for her
rustic surroundings. His dismissing glance flicked over
the stained sink, the old iron daybed bolstered to double
as a sofa, and the faded curtain that served as a door to
the sleeping nook.

He dipped his head at the grocery bags. "Where do
you want these?"

Lacey moved to clear a space on the old pine table,
shifting a stack of books, a sketch pad, a box of pastels
and some pencils to one of the four ladderback chairs.
"Right here." She pulled the chain on the bulb sus-
pended over the table. The resulting wash of light was
harsh, but functional.

Logan moved forward and slid the groceries onto the

table, then stepped back. They regarded each other. She saw that there were circles under those fine dark eyes of his.

Was it only the severity of the light? No. Now that she stared directly at him, she could see more than irritated disapproval in the sculpted planes of his face. She saw weariness. Reproach and concern were there, too.

She cleared her throat and spoke gently. "Did you drive all the way from California?"

He shook his head. "I flew out of Reno. To Denver, where I transferred to a smaller plane, which got me to Sheridan. Then I rented a car for the rest of the trip."

"You must be tired."

His mouth tightened. She read the hidden meaning in his expression. He'd come to take care of her, whether she liked it or not. His own comfort was nothing. "I'm fine."

"Well. I'm glad to hear it."

The silence stretched out again. Maybe he was thirsty. "Do you want something to drink?"

He shrugged, then answered with a formality that tugged at her heart. "Yes. Thank you. Something cold would be good."

"Ginger ale?"

"That's fine."

She went to the refrigerator, which was probably a collector's item—it stood on legs and had a coil on top. She took out a can, then turned to the cabinet over the one tiny section of counter.

"Never mind a glass," he said. "Just the can is fine."

She handed it to him across the table, absurdly conscious of the possibility that their fingers might brush in passing. They didn't.

She gestured at the chair in front of him. "Have a seat."

He ignored that suggestion, popped the top on the can and took a long drink.

She stared at his Adam's apple as it bobbed up and down on his strong, tanned throat and tried to ignore the yearning that flooded through her in a warm, tempting wave.

She wanted him.

Even big as a cow with the baby they had created together, she'd have happily sashayed right over to him and put her mouth against that brown throat. With delight, she would have teasingly scraped the skin with her teeth, stuck out her tongue and tasted—

Lacey cut off the dangerous erotic thought before it could get too good a hold on her very healthy imagination. As if she even *could* sashay, big as she'd grown in the last month or so.

Logan set the ginger ale can on the table. "How long have you been here?"

"Seven weeks."

He waited, clearly expecting her to elaborate. When she didn't, he asked, softly, "Why?"

She looked away, realized she'd done it, and made herself face him again. "Why not? This ranch has been in my family for five generations. My second cousin, Zach, runs the place now."

"That doesn't answer my question. What made you choose to come here?"

"Jenna suggested it." As Lacey said her sister's

name, it became clear to her that she'd been avoiding saying it. For her own sake or for Logan's, she couldn't be sure. But the name was out now. And the world hadn't stopped. "She and Mack stayed here for a few weeks last year."

There. She had said *both* of the dangerous names. Jenna and Mack. The woman Logan loved. And the man who had taken her from him.

Lacey watched for his reaction. If he had one, he wasn't sharing it. His face remained composed. He didn't even blink.

"Jenna knows—about you and me?" His voice was cautious, but resigned.

"Yes."

"She knows that the baby is mine?"

Lacey nodded. "I told her about you and me not too long after it happened—and about the baby a few months ago. She wanted me to go and stay with her and Mack in Florida for the birth."

"Why didn't you?"

Lacey stared at him. Did he really want to hear the answer to that one? Apparently he did, or he would not have been so foolish as to ask.

She shrugged. "I didn't want to intrude on their happiness." Jenna and Mack were like newlyweds, having recently reunited after years apart. "And Jenna is pregnant, too. Her baby is due in September."

Logan glanced down at the table between them. He might have been looking at the bags of groceries, or the empty soda can—or simply *not* looking at her. "Well," he said, "Jenna always did want lots of kids."

"Yes. She did."

Logan raised that dark gaze once more. "So you came here."

Lacey nodded. "It's peaceful and it's beautiful. And I have family around, ready to help if I need it. It was the perfect place to come and have my baby."

He let a moment of charged silence elapse before announcing, "You should have come to me."

Well, she thought. *We're into it now, aren't we?* She knew where he was headed, of course. She'd known from the moment she saw him on the front step. And even before that. She'd known what Logan Severance would do from the first day she admitted to herself that she was pregnant—because she knew *him.*

And she had her refusal, complete with excellent reasons for it, all ready to give to him.

But the thought of hashing through it all made her feel about as tired as he looked. And her back was aching.

If he wanted to stand up for this, fine. He could stand. She'd rather take it sitting down.

Lacey pulled out a chair and lowered herself into it.

Logan waited to speak again until she was settled—and until it became clear that she wasn't going to respond to his last remark. "The baby's due in a week or so, right?"

"Yes." Her shoulders kept wanting to droop. She pulled them back and met his eyes. "Everything's fine. Normal. I got an appointment with the doctor here as soon as I arrived. He's been taking good care of me."

Logan looked irritatingly skeptical. "You've been watching your diet, taking it easy?"

Oh, why did he so often manage to make her feel like

some incompetent, irresponsible child? Apparently, old behavior patterns did die hard. In spite of the dramatic shift in their relationship last fall, right that moment the years seemed to peel away. She was the bratty kid with a chip on her shoulder and he was the annoyingly straight-arrow boyfriend of her big sister.

"Lacey. Answer me. Have you been taking care of yourself?"

"Honestly, everything is fine."

That gained her a disbelieving glare. "Why didn't you contact me earlier?"

"I contacted you as soon as I could bear to. And if we're into 'why didn't you,' then why didn't you call the number I gave you and let me know that you were on your way here?"

"And have you tell me not to come? I don't think so."

Her mouth felt so dry all of a sudden. It was one of the many bothersome things about pregnancy. Cravings came on out of nowhere. She wanted water. She could already taste its silky coldness on her tongue. She started to push herself to her feet again.

Logan frowned. "What is it?"

"Nothing. I just want a drink of water, that's all."

"I'll get it."

"No, don't bother. I can—"

But he was already striding to the sink. He took a glass from the corner of the counter, rinsed it, and filled it from the tap. Then he carried it to her and held it out.

She looked at the glass and then up, into his eyes. His kindness and concern did touch her. He was a good man, always had been. Much too good for the likes of her. She felt a smile flirting with the corners of her mouth. "You know, until a few years ago, there was no running water or electricity here in the cabin. It cost a bundle, apparently, to run electrical lines and water pipes out here. But my cousin Zach had it done last summer. Pretty convenient, huh? Otherwise, you'd have had to head for the well out back to fill that glass for me."

"Just drink." His voice was gruff.

This time, as he passed her the glass, his fingers did brush hers. His fingers were warm. She wondered if hers felt cold to him.

"Thank you." She drank. It was just what she'd wanted, clear and cool and satisfying as it slid down her throat.

"More?"

She shook her head, set down the glass.

Logan pulled out the chair nearest hers and dropped into it. He braced his elbows on his knees and leaned toward her. The light caught and gleamed in his dark hair.

His eyes were softer now. "I didn't call when I got your letter because I knew you would only try to talk me into staying away."

Her smile started to quiver. She bit the corner of her lip to make it stop. "That's true. I would have."

"It wouldn't have worked."

"I know. You'll do what you think is right. You always have." Except during those five days last September, a voice in her mind whispered tauntingly. *Then you did things you didn't approve of. And you did them with me.*

He looked down at the rough boards between his

feet, then back up at her. "This baby changes everything, Lace."

She wanted to touch him. The slight brushing of their fingers a moment before had whetted her appetite for the feel of him. Oh, to simply reach out and run her fingers through that shining dark hair, to trace his brows, to learn again the shape of his mouth.

Tenderness welled in her. He had traveled such a long way and he wasn't going to get what he came for—what he would say he wanted, what he would call the right thing.

He said it then, as if he had plucked the words right out of her mind. "We have to do the right thing now."

She sat back in her chair and clasped her hands beneath the hard swell of her belly. "Your idea of the right thing and mine are not the same, Logan."

He answered her with measured care. "The right thing is the right thing, period."

"Fine. Whatever. The point is, I'm not going to marry you."

Chapter 2

Logan had pretty much expected this. He straightened in the chair and kept his voice level and reasonable. "Before you turn me down flat, let's discuss this a little. You're in no position to raise a child on your own, and I'm willing to—"

"Logan, I told you. No. It's a two-letter word meaning negative, out of the question. Uh-uh. Forgetaboutit." She pushed herself to her feet. "We are not getting married."

"Why not?"

She stared at him for a moment, then made a show of hitting her forehead with the heel of her hand. "What? You can't figure that one out for yourself?"

"Spare me the theatrics. Just answer the question. Why not?"

Muttering under her breath, she turned to her gro-

ceries, grabbed a box of Wheat Thins in one hand and
a can of cocoa mix in the other and started toward the
ancient wood-burning stove that crouched against the
wall by the front door.

His frustration with her got the better of him. "Sit
down," he commanded.

It was the wrong thing to say, and he knew it. But
something about Lacey Bravo tended to bring out the
tyrant in him.

Why was that? He had no idea. He considered himself a reasonable, gentle man, as a rule. He *was* a reasonable, gentle man as a rule. Ask just about anyone
who knew him.

Lacey ignored his command. She reached the stove
and put the crackers and cocoa mix on the open shelf
above it. Then she turned for the table again and shuffled his way, her abdomen heavy and low in front of
her—low enough, in fact, to make him suspect that the
baby inside her had already dropped toward the birth
canal.

It could be *less* than a week before she brought his
child into the world.

They needed to get married.

She reached into the bag again. He stood. "Lace.
Stop. You know we have to talk about this."

She took her hand out of the bag and raked that thick
gold hair of hers back from her forehead. "Not about
marriage, we don't."

"I disagree. I think marriage is exactly what we do
need to talk about. I think that—"

She put up both hands, palms out. "Wait. Listen.
You're the baby's father. And of course, you'll want to

see him or her, to be a part of his life. I understand that and I can accept that. But it really isn't necessary for you to—"

"It damn well *is* necessary. You're having my baby and a baby needs a mother *and* a father."

"I told you. The baby *will* have a mother and a father. They just won't be married to each other, that's all."

"A two-parent home is important to a child."

"Sometimes a two-parent home isn't possible."

"In our case, it's entirely possible. I want to marry you. We're both single. I make a good living and I do care for you. I believe that, deep in your heart, you also care for me. I know I'm rough on you sometimes, rougher than I have a right to be. But I'll work on that, I promise you."

She said nothing, only looked at him, shaking her head.

He thought of more arguments in his favor. "We have…history together. I feel I really *know* you, that you really know me. We could build a good life together, I'm sure of it."

Still, she didn't speak.

A grotesque thought occurred to him. "Is there another man? Is that it?"

She closed her eyes and sucked in a breath.

He realized that, if there was another man, he didn't want to know. Which was irrational. Of course, if there was someone else, he needed to know.

He asked again. "Lace? Is there another man?"

"No," she said in a tiny, soft voice. "No one. There hasn't been anyone. Since you. Since quite a while before you, if you want to know the truth."

Relief shimmered through him. "Good. Then there's nothing to stop you from marrying me."

She backed up and let herself down into the chair again. "How can you say that?"

"Lace—"

"No, Logan. I am not going to marry you." She looked up at him, blue eyes glittering in defiance, mulishly determined to do exactly the wrong thing.

Impatience rose in him again. "Why not?"

She glared at him. "You keep asking that. Do you really want an answer? Do you really want me to say it right out?"

He didn't.

But he wasn't about to tell her that. She'd only look at him as if he'd just proved her point.

"Let me put it this way," she said with heavy irony. "If I ever do get married, it won't be to a man who's in love with my big sister."

He tried not to flinch as the words came at him.

And he did realize the opportunity they presented. Now was his chance to tell her firmly that he was not in love with Jenna. But somehow, he couldn't quite get the denial out of his mouth.

Lacey smiled sadly, shook her head some more, and murmured his name in a knowing way that made him want to grab her and flip her over his knee and paddle her behind until she admitted he was right and accepted his proposal. Until she confessed how glad she was that he had come at last, that he was ready, willing and able to make everything right.

Lacey wasn't confessing anything. She said, "I have my own plans. I'm staying here in Wyoming until the baby's born and I'm back on my feet. Then I'll return to L.A."

Absurd, he thought. Impossible. And harebrained, as well. "You can't be serious. There is no way you can support both yourself and a child on what you make working odd jobs and selling a painting every now and then."

"We'll get by. Jenna and I sold our mother's house. I have money put aside from that, and a new car, so the baby and I will be able to get around. In fact, I have everything I need." Her full, soft mouth stretched into a smile—a rather forced one this time. "And besides, I know you'll help out."

He reminded himself that he would not lose his patience again. She had always been like this. Impetuous and wild. Running away whenever things didn't go her way. A virtual delinquent as a teenager, hanging out with all the troublemakers at Meadow Valley High. And then, at twenty, taking off for Los Angeles to study under some famous painter, sure she would "make it" as an artist. Six years had gone by since then. She hadn't made it yet.

Now she proposed to drag his baby to Southern California to scrape and starve right along with her.

It wasn't going to happen. "I'll help out, all right," he said. "We'll get married. You'll live with me. You can paint your paintings in Meadow Valley just as well as in L.A."

"I said no, Logan. And I meant it."

He folded his arms across his chest—mostly to keep himself from reaching out and strangling her. "This isn't last September. You can't just explain to me how

I don't love you and I'm only on the rebound from your sister and it's time we both moved on."

"You happened to agree with me last September, in case you've forgotten."

Had he agreed with her? Maybe. He'd been confused as hell last September. Hard to remember now *what* he had felt then.

Jenna had left with Mack McGarrity.

And then, out of nowhere, her little sister, who had always irritated the hell out of him, showed up on his doorstep, real concern for him in her gorgeous blue eyes and a big chocolate cake in her hands.

"You need chocolate, Dr. Do-Right," she had said. "Lots of chocolate. And you need it now."

Dr. Do-Right. He hated it when she called him that. He had opened his mouth to tell her so—and also to tell her to please go away.

But she just pushed past him and kept walking, straight to his kitchen. She put the cake on the counter and began rifling the drawers. It didn't take her long to find the one with the silverware in it.

"Ah," she said. "Here we go." She grabbed a fork, shoved the drawer shut and thrust the fork at him, catching him off guard, so that he took it automatically. "Eat."

He looked at the fork and he looked at the cake.

Damned if she didn't know just what he was thinking. "No," she said. "No plate. No nice little slice cut with a knife. Just stick that fork right in there, just tear off a big, gooey bite."

He stared at her, stared at her full mouth, at her flushed face, her wide eyes…

And he realized that he was aroused.

Aroused by Jenna's troublemaking little sister, damned if he wasn't.

He had set down the fork, backed her up against the counter and spoken right into that deceptively angelic face of hers. "Shouldn't you be back in L.A. by now?"

Her breathing was agitated, though she tried to play it cool. "I told Jenna I'd take care of things here."

"I don't need taking care of."

She didn't say anything, just looked at him through those blue, blue eyes.

"You'd better go," he had warned.

She made a small, tender sound.

And she shook her head.

They ate the cake sometime after midnight, both of them nude, standing in the kitchen, tearing into it with a pair of forks, then feeding each other big, sloppy bites.

Lacey shifted in her chair. Logan's eyes looked far away. She wondered what he was thinking.

He blinked and came back to himself. "I don't want to analyze last September. It happened. We weren't as careful as we should have been and now you're having my baby. You know damn well how I feel about that."

Yes, she did know. He was just like Jenna. He wanted children. Several children. He also wanted a nice, settled, stay-at-home wife to take care of those children while he was out healing the ills of the world. A wife like Jenna would have been.

In almost every way, Logan and Jenna had been just right for each other. Too bad Jenna had always loved Mack McGarrity.

Logan held out his hand.

Lacey knew that she shouldn't, but she took it anyway. He pulled her out of the chair. He would have taken her into his arms, but she resisted that.

Her belly brushed him. They both hitched in a quick breath at the contact and Lacey pulled her hand from his.

She turned toward the table, toward the grocery bags still waiting there, thinking that the move might gain her a little much-needed distance from him.

It didn't. He stepped up behind her, so that she could feel him, feel the warmth of him, close at her back.

He spoke into her ear, his voice barely a whisper. "You need me now, Lace. Don't turn me away. Give me a chance. I want to marry you and take care of you…of both of you."

Oh, those *were* lovely words. And, yes, they did tempt her.

But it wouldn't work. She had to remember that. It couldn't work.

He did not love her. He couldn't even say that he no longer loved her sister. He'd marry her out of duty, in order to claim his child.

And she would spend her life with him feeling like second best, wondering when he kissed her if he was imagining her sister in his arms. She didn't want that. They had too many differences as it was. Without love on both sides, they wouldn't stand a chance.

Gently, he took her shoulder, the touch burning a path of longing down inside of her, making her sigh. He turned her to face him.

And he smiled. "I'm feeling pretty determined, Lace."

She smiled right back at him. "So am I."

"We'll see who's *more* determined of the two of us. I'm not going away until you come with me."

"Then you're in for a long stay in Wyoming."

"I can stay as long as I have to."

"You couldn't stay long enough."

"Watch me."

"What about your practice? How will your patients get along without you?"

"Don't worry about my patients. I have partners to cover for me. I can stick it out here for as long as it takes."

"Oh? And where will you be staying? Have you made reservations at the motel in town?"

"No. I'll stay here with you."

He looked so certain, so set on his goal. She couldn't stop herself. She touched the side of his face. The stubble-rough skin felt wonderful—*too* wonderful.

She jerked her hand back, thinking how much one thoughtless touch could do. In a moment, she'd have no backbone left. Whatever he wanted, she'd just go along.

"You can't stay here," she said in a breathless tone that convinced neither Logan nor herself. "It's out of the question."

He pressed his advantage. "Look. You're alone here. The baby's due any day now. I don't even see a phone in this cabin. How will you call for help if there's an emergency?"

She tipped her chin higher. "I'm in no danger. The

main ranch house is nearby—you must have driven past it to get here."

He nodded. "I stopped in there for directions, as a matter of fact. And it's too far away. You could have trouble reaching it, if something went really wrong."

"I have a cell phone. I can call for help if I need to."

"You're telling me that a cell phone actually works out here?"

"Yes."

He made a small chiding noise. "Not very dependably, though. I can see it in your eyes."

"It doesn't matter. I'm perfectly safe here."

"Not in your condition. You know you shouldn't be alone."

He was starting to sound way too much like her cousin. Zach—and Tess, too—had been nagging her constantly of late, trying to get her to move to the main house now that her due date was so close. She kept putting them off.

She did plan on moving, as soon as the baby came. Tess already had a room ready for the two of them, with a nice big bed for her, and a bassinet and a changing table and everything else that the baby would need.

But right now, Lacey felt she was managing well enough. And the cabin did please her. She had music— a boom box and a pile of CDs in the sleeping nook. She read a lot and she sketched all the time. Lately, since just before she'd come to Wyoming, she'd discovered that she no longer had the kind of total concentration it took to work seriously on a painting. But that was all right. She sensed that it would come back to her, after the baby arrived—no matter what Xavier Hockland, her former teacher and mentor, chose to believe.

And certainly she could manage to make it to the main house when her labor began. Tess could take her to the hospital from there.

Logan began prowling around the room. He stopped by the big stove. "What do you use to heat this place?"

"Wood. Lately, the weather's so mild, I hardly need heat, though. And if I do, I only have to build one fire, in the morning. By the time it burns down, it's warm outside."

"How do you cook?"

"Same thing. I build a fire."

"You're chopping wood in your condition?"

She made a face at him. "No. Zach takes care of it. He keeps the wood bin out in back nice and full."

"But you have to haul it in here and build the fire yourself?"

"It's not that difficult, Logan."

"Heavy lifting is a bad idea at this point. Your doctor should have told you that."

"Logan. Come on. Stop picking on sweet old Doc Pruitt. I only carry in a few pieces of wood at a time. There honestly is no heavy lifting involved."

He marched over to her again. "You need help around here. And even if you won't marry me, I think I have a right to be here when my baby is born."

She opened her mouth to rebut that—and then shut it without making a sound. He was right. If he wanted to be here for the birth of their child, who was she to deny him?

"Who knows?" he added. "You might even need a

doctor in a hurry. Then you'd be doubly glad that I stuck around."

Score one more for his side. She could go into labor any time now. If, God forbid, anything should go wrong before she reached the hospital in Buffalo, it wouldn't hurt to have a doctor at her side.

And who was she kidding, anyway?

Beyond the issues of her isolation in the cabin, of a father's rights and Logan's skills as a physician, there was her foolish heart, beating too hard under her breastbone, just waiting for any excuse to keep him near for a while.

It astonished her now, to look back on all those years growing up, when the name Logan Severance had inspired in her a feeling of profound irritation at best. Logan Severance, her sister's perfect, straight-A boyfriend, who played halfback on the high school football team, took honors in debate and went to University of California in Davis on full scholarship. Logan Severance, who seemed to think it was his duty to whip his sweetheart's messed-up little sister into shape. He was always after her to stand up straight, carping at her about her grades, lecturing her when she ran away or got caught stealing bubble gum from Mr. Kretchmeir's corner store.

Sometimes, she had actually thought that she hated him.

But not anymore.

Now she knew that she loved him. She had figured that out last September, on the fifth glorious day of their crazy, impossible affair. It turned out to be the last day. As soon as she admitted the grim truth to herself, she had seen the self-defeating hopelessness of what she was doing. She had told him she couldn't see him anymore.

He had called her three times after she returned to L.A. She'd found his messages on her answering machine and played each of them back over and over, until they had burned themselves a permanent place in her brain. She had memorized each word, each breath, each nuance of sound...

"Hello, Lacey. It's Logan. I was just—listen. Why don't you give me a call?"

"Lacey. Logan. I left a message a month ago. Did you get it? Are you all right? Sometimes I... Never mind. I suppose I should just leave you alone."

"Lace. It's Logan. If you don't call me back this time, I won't try again."

She had started to call him a hundred times. And she had always put the phone down before she went through with it, though she had known by his second call that she was carrying his baby, known that eventually she would make herself tell him.

Known he would come to her as soon as she did.

And that once he came, it would be harder than ever to send him away.

He smoothed a coil of hair back from her cheek. She savored the lovely, light caress.

He murmured so tenderly, "Say I can stay."

She put off giving in. "I don't want to hear any more talk about marriage. It's out of the question, Logan. Do you understand?"

His eyes gleamed in satisfaction. "That's a yes, right?"

"Not to marriage."

"But you'll let me stay here with you."

"Just until the baby's born. After that, you have to go. We can make arrangements for you to see the baby on a regular basis, and we can—"

He put a finger against her lips. "Shh. There's no need to worry about all that now."

She pulled her head back, away from the touch of that finger of his. It was too tempting by half, that finger. She might just get foolish and suck it right inside her mouth.

His grin seemed terribly smug.

She told him so. "I do not like the look on your face."

"What look?" He reached for one of the grocery bags. "Come on. I'll help you put this stuff away."

Chapter 3

As soon as the shopping bags were emptied, Logan went out and got his things from the car. There was only one bureau in the dark little cabin. A scarred mahogany monstrosity with a streaked mirror on top. It loomed against the wall by the rear door, sandwiched between a pair of crammed-full pine bookcases. Lacey gave him three of the eight drawers. He'd traveled light, so everything fit in the space she assigned him.

As he unpacked, Lacey sat in the old rocker in the corner, watching him, rocking slowly, her abdomen a hard mound taking up most of her lap, her head resting back, those blue eyes drooping a little.

When he finished, he shoved his empty bag and extra shoes under the daybed. Then he dropped onto the mattress, which was covered with a patchwork quilt. "That's that."

"Umm," she said softly. The rocker creaked as she idly moved it back and forth.

He leaned an elbow on the ironwork bedstead and allowed himself the luxury of just looking at her.

She looked good. Her skin glowed with health and her golden hair still possessed the glossy sheen he remembered. Pregnancy seemed to agree with her. That pleased him. He wanted more children, after this one. A whole house full. It wouldn't be the way it had been when he was a boy, just him and his father and the endless string of housekeepers who had never managed to take the place that should have been filled by a wife and mother.

His kids would have more than that. His kids would have brothers and sisters—and both of their parents. There would be noise and laughter and a feeling of belonging.

Lacey went on rocking—and she smiled.

He wanted to touch her, to put his hand on the fine, smooth skin of her cheek, to run it down over her throat and then over her breasts, which looked sweet and firm and full, even beneath the shapeless denim dress she wore. He wanted to spread both hands on her belly, test the hardness of it now, when she was so close to term, maybe even get lucky and feel his baby kick.

But he knew she wouldn't allow such intimate explorations of her body. Not now. Not so soon after he'd forced himself back into her life.

He was going to have to wait to have his hands on her. Probably until after he had managed to convince her to marry him.

Well, fair enough. He'd waited nine months, telling

himself most of the time that this physical yearning he felt for Jenna's little sister would eventually pass.

It hadn't. And recently he'd allowed himself to accept the fact that it was only Mother Nature playing at irony.

Lacey Bravo, of all people, was his sexual ideal.

Explain it? He couldn't, didn't really even care to. Human beings were primates, after all, aroused by things they didn't consciously understand. By certain scents and secretions. Desire had nothing at all to do with logic. It was a chemical reaction, the natural attraction of one healthy specimen for another, designed to perpetuate the species.

Now that Lacey was having his baby and he meant to marry her, he found it a real bonus that he wanted her so much. They might have their problems in a lot of different areas, but he didn't think sex was going to be one of them.

She stopped rocking and lifted her head off the backrest. "Are you tired?"

He almost said no. But then he reconsidered. He could use a nap, as a matter of fact. He'd been up well before dawn. And he hadn't been getting much sleep in the last week anyway, not since her letter had arrived.

"A little," he said. "I'll lie down for a while if you will, too." He wanted to make certain she got plenty of rest.

"It's a deal." She put both hands on the rocker arms and levered herself to a standing position.

He asked, in a tone as offhand as he could make it, "Is there a double bed behind that curtain?"

She gave him a lazy grin. "Nice try. You get the

daybed." She shuffled out the back door. After a few minutes, he heard the toilet flush. She came back in, only to disappear behind the curtain in the corner.

He paid a short visit to the bathroom himself, then took off his shoes and lay down. Like every other piece of furniture in the cabin, the bed appeared to be something salvaged from an earlier era. It had creaky springs and a lumpy mattress and it wasn't long enough to fully accommodate his six-foot-three-inch frame. But he stretched out as best he could, letting his stocking feet hang over the edge and pulling one of the long sausage-shaped bolster pillows under his head.

A strange kind of peace settled over him, a deep relaxation, a sense of well-being. It was a state he hadn't experienced in a long time. He dropped off to sleep like a rock falling down a well.

The next thing he knew, someone was knocking on the door.

Logan bolted to a sitting position, blinking and staring around him, wondering where the hell he was.

Then it all fell into place. The long trip from California. To this cabin. In Wyoming. Lacey. Pregnant with his baby. She was resting now, on the other side of that curtain over there. He glanced at his Rolex. She'd been in there for less than an hour.

And whatever idiot had dropped in for a visit would probably wake her with the next knock.

He jumped to his feet and padded swiftly to the door. When he pulled it open, he found a cowboy on the other side. Behind the cowboy, hitched to one of the poles that held up the porch, a handsome horse with a reddish-brown coat let out a low snort and flicked his shiny tail at a couple of flies.

The cowboy lifted his hat in greeting, then settled it back on his head. "I'm Zach Bravo." His gaze shifted down, paused on Logan's stocking feet, then quickly shifted up again. "Just thought I'd stop by and check on things out here."

"Logan?" It was Lacey's voice, sounding slow and sleepy, from the other end of the room. "Who is it?" She stood just beyond the curtain in the corner, her feet bare, her face soft and her hair mussed from sleep.

"It's Zach," said the cowboy, craning to see around Logan, who had positioned himself squarely in the open doorway.

Lacey grinned and started toward them. "Come on in. I can probably scare up a beer if you want one."

Zach Bravo stayed where he was. "No. Got to get a move on. Never enough hours in a day around here. But Tess asked me to see if you wanted to come over to the house for dinner tonight. Around six?"

Logan stepped aside a little as Lacey came up next to him. "Zach, this is Dr. Logan Severance, a…dear friend." Logan didn't miss her slight hesitation over what to call him. He'd bet his license to practice medicine that Zach Bravo didn't miss it either.

"Pleased to meet you." The rancher held out a tough brown hand.

Logan took it, gave it a firm shake. "The pleasure is mine."

"You'll come for dinner then…both of you?"

Lacey lifted an eyebrow at Logan. He nodded and she smiled at her cousin. "We'll be there. Six o'clock."

"So I'm your dear friend," Logan challenged the minute Zach Bravo had mounted his horse and trotted away down the dirt road that led to the cluster of ranch buildings just over the next rise.

Lacey made a noise in her throat. "What should I have said? Former lover? The father of my child?"

"How about husband?"

"But that wouldn't be true, now, would it?"

"We could make it true."

She looked at him for a long, cool moment, then announced defiantly, "Zach comes out to check on me two or three times a day, which is just another reason why I'm perfectly safe on my own here."

"I'd say he came to check on *me* this time."

"Right. He's protective. More proof that I'm in no danger at all, as I've constantly tried to make you realize. You simply do not have to stay in this cabin with me. If you want to be here when the baby's born, you could take a room in the motel in town and—"

"I'm not leaving, Lacey—and your cousin strikes me as a conservative man, the kind of man who would feel a lot better if you were married to the father of your child."

She put her hands on her hips. "You are truly relentless. Now we should get married so as not to offend Zach's conservative sensibilities?"

"I'm only pointing out that—"

"Logan. You said you would drop it."

Lacey gave him her best unwavering stare. She was wondering, as she had more than once in the past nine months, how she could love such an obnoxious man.

He stared right back, which forced her to demand, "Are you dropping it, Logan?"

He made a growling sound. "All right, all right. I'm dropping it."

"Good."

His handsome face had settled into a scowl. She watched him rearrange it to something more gentle. "We've got another hour and a half before we have to make our appearance at your cousin's house. Why don't you go on back behind that curtain and lie down again?"

She blew a tangled curl out of her eye. "No, thanks. I'm wide awake now." She marched to the sleeping nook, ducked inside and came out with her lace-up hiking boots.

His eyes narrowed with suspicion. "What are you doing?"

She sat in the rocker and pulled on one of the boots. It wasn't easy, working around the bulge of her stomach, but she'd had a lot of practice in the past few weeks. Huffing and puffing, she tied the boot, pulled on the other one, tied it up, too.

"Lacey."

She stood, turned to the bureau, picked up the brush lying on top and went to work on her hair. Their eyes met in the mirror. "I'm going out behind the cabin a ways. There's a creek that runs by back there. Very picturesque. I've been doing a few sketches. Willows and cottonwoods, a few cows and their calves..." He was scowling again. She pretended not to notice. "I'll be back in an hour or so, in plenty of time for dinner with Zach and Tess and the family."

"Are you sure that you should—?"

She turned and pointed the brush at him. "Don't, all right? Just…don't. Nothing's going to happen to me down by the creek. It's barely a hundred yards from the back door, for heaven's sake."

"What if some big bull comes at you?"

"It's not an issue."

"This is a cattle ranch, isn't it? If I'm not mistaken, bulls live on cattle ranches."

She struggled to contain her building exasperation. "There's a barbed-wire fence that runs between this particular spot on the creek and those cattle I mentioned. If there are any bulls nearby, they would most likely be on the other side of that fence."

"But—"

"Read my lips. I'll be fine."

"I'll come with—"

"Logan. Stop. If you insist on staying here, in a twenty-by-twenty-foot space with me, we're going to have to give each other a little breathing room. I am going alone."

He shut his mouth, made another growling sound and then dropped to the side of the daybed. "Great. Fine. Do what you want to do. You never in your life did anything else." He braced his elbows on his spread knees and shook his head at his stocking feet.

Tenderness washed through her. She set down the brush. "You're the one who needs more rest. Come on. Stretch out and sleep for an hour. You'll have the cabin all to yourself. Forget all your cares and I'll wake you up when I get back."

He didn't say anything, just went on staring at his socks.

"Logan..."

"All right. I'll take a damn nap." He lay down on his back with his feet over the edge, turned his face to the wall and shut his eyes.

Smiling to herself, Lacey collected her sketch pad and a couple of nice, soft pencils from the chair where she'd set them earlier. Before she went out, she couldn't resist whispering, "Sleep well."

"Thanks," he grumbled, neither turning his head nor opening his eyes. "Be careful, for God's sake."

"I will, Logan. I promise you."

He was sound asleep when she returned, lying in almost the same position she'd left him in, his hands folded on his chest. His head, however, was turned toward the room now.

Lacey stood over him, admiring the beauty of his body in repose, thinking that maybe she could do a few sketches of him sleeping—nothing too challenging right now. She wasn't up for it. But she could certainly line out a few ideas in pencil.

Then, later, after the baby came, she could go back to what she'd started, delve more deeply. She loved the softness of his face when he was sleeping. And something else. Some...determined vulnerability. Some aspect of his will that came through even when he was unconscious, some sense that he distrusted the necessity of surrendering to sleep.

He had a wonderful face, handsome in a classic way. And very masculine—she'd always thought so, even before she realized she was in love with him. A broad forehead, a strongly defined supraorbital arch, so the eyes were set deep, shadowed in their sockets. Cheekbones and jawline were clean and clear-cut and his finely shaped mouth possessed just enough softness to betray the sensuality she'd discovered with such delight during their five incredible days together last fall.

Though he didn't know it, she had painted him. A number of nudes, from memory, in the first months after their affair. She believed they were her best work so far. And she had exercised great ingenuity, in all of them, so as not to reveal his face.

Had she been wrong to paint him without his knowledge? After all, Logan Severance was not the kind of man who posed for nude studies—let alone the kind who would allow them to be hung in an art gallery for all the world to see. Those paintings weren't in any gallery yet. But someday they would be. Lacey had told herself that she'd protected his privacy by obscuring his face. But sometimes she felt just a little bit guilty about them, wondered what his reaction would be if he ever saw them—which he would probably have to. Someday.

She wasn't particularly looking forward to that day.

"What are you staring at?"

Caught thoroughly off guard, Lacey gasped and stepped back. She could have sworn he was sound asleep just seconds ago. But those eyes looking into hers now were clear and alert.

"Well?"

The truth slipped out—or at least, some of it. "I was thinking that I'd like to sketch you while you're sleeping."

"Why?"

"Something in your face. Something…unguarded, but unwillingly so. It's very appealing."

He grinned. "You like me best unconscious, is that what you're telling me?"

She'd regained her composure enough to reply smartly, "I wouldn't have put it that way, but now that you've done it yourself…"

"Marry me. You can watch me sleep for the rest of our lives."

She resolutely did not respond to that. "We should go. It's quarter of six."

At the big side-gabled wood frame ranch house, Zach introduced his family to Logan.

"This is Tess." He put his arm around his wife. "And our daughters, Starr and Jobeth."

The older of the two girls, a beauty of about eighteen, with black hair and Elizabeth Taylor eyes, gave him a polite "Hello." The younger one, Jobeth, who looked ten or eleven, smiled shyly and nodded.

Next, Logan shook Edna Heller's slim, fine-boned hand and learned that she had once been the ranch's housekeeper but now was one of the family; her only daughter had married a Bravo cousin, Cash. She lived in the foreman's cottage, which was just across the drive from the main house.

"And this is Ethan John," Tess said. She held up a big, healthy blue-eyed baby. "Ethan is just six months old today." The baby gurgled out something that sounded almost like a greeting.

They ate at the long table in the Bravos' formal

dining room. Ethan John sat in his high chair and chewed on a teething ring and occasionally let out a happy, crowing laugh.

"Ethan's already had his dinner," Tess explained. "We enjoy having him with us during meals, but we don't enjoy watching the food fly. So I feed him early and he sits with us and everybody's happy." Tess turned her smile on Logan. "Do you have children, Mr. Severance?"

Logan answered that one carefully. "Not yet."

"You plan to, then?"

He sent a significant glance at Lacey, who was sitting directly to his left. She smiled at him, an innocent, what-are-you-looking-at-me-for? smile. Apparently, he was on his own here.

"Yes," he said. "I plan to have children…very soon."

Now it was Zach and Tess's turn to trade glances. And the two girls, as well. They looked at their parents first, then swapped a glance of their own. Edna Heller somehow managed to make eye contact with all four of the others. She shared knowing looks with Zach and Tess, and right after that flashed a "mind your business, girls," expression at their daughters.

Lacey was grinning. Apparently she thought the whole exchange of meaningful looks rather amusing.

Logan didn't. As far as he was concerned, those flying glances were just more proof that Lacey needed to come to her senses and marry him immediately. It was an embarrassment to sit here with this nice family and have them all wonder what the hell was going on between their unmarried pregnant cousin and the strange man who'd shown up out of nowhere this afternoon—and appeared to have set up housekeeping with her.

He wanted to get the truth out in the open. He wanted to say bluntly, That's my baby Lacey's carrying and I've come to marry her and take her home with me where she belongs.

But he couldn't do that. Not here at the Bravo dinner table, with a girl of Jobeth's age listening in.

"How do you and Lacey know each other?" asked Edna Heller. She was a small, slender woman, probably in her fifties, and very feminine—though in her eyes Logan could see a glint of steel. Not much would get by her.

She was smiling at him in the most polite way and waiting for an answer. Unfortunately, the truth wouldn't sound good at all. *I've been in love with Lacey's sister since I was eighteen years old. Jenna was going to marry me—until she decided to run off with Mack McGarrity instead.*

Lacey came to his rescue on that one. "Logan and Jenna went to school together. Logan's been sort of a big brother figure to me over the years."

Edna Heller's eyebrows rose daintily toward her hairline. "Ah. A big brother figure."

"He's always felt he has to take care of me. He still feels that way. Don't you, Logan?"

"That's right."

"That's…admirable of you, Mr. Severance."

"Thank you, Mrs. Heller."

"You know, for years my son-in-law, Cash, imagined himself a big brother to my Abigail. But then he married her and found out he was deeply in love with her. Abigail, of course, always worshipped him."

"Oh, really?" Logan said, for lack of something better to say.

Lacey couldn't let Edna's observation go unchallenged. "Are we supposed to be noting similarities between Cash and Abby—and Logan and me?"

"Well," said Edna airily. "Only if the shoe fits, as they say."

"The shoe does not fit. Logan and I are not getting married. And if you ask him, he'll tell you he never got any worship from me."

Edna might give the Bravo daughters stern looks admonishing them to stay out of others' affairs, but she clearly thought of herself as someone who had a right to be in the know. She turned to Logan. "Well, Mr. Severance?"

Lacey hasn't fully accepted the idea yet, but we are getting married, he thought. He said, "No. Worship is not the word I would use to describe Lacey's feelings for me."

"What word would you use, then?"

He shrugged. "Let's just say it wouldn't be worship and leave it at that."

There was a silence, which was quickly filled with nonsense syllables from the baby and the clink of silver against china plates.

Zach said, "More potatoes, Logan?"

"Yes, please. This is a terrific meal, Tess."

Tess colored prettily at the compliment. "Well, I must confess. Edna always does the potatoes around here. I swear she has a way of making them light enough that they could get right up and float off your plate."

Edna smiled graciously—and went back to her velvet-gloved interrogation. "And how long will you be staying on the Rising Sun, Mr. Severance?"

He shot a look at Lacey. She'd had a lot to say a minute ago. Maybe she'd want to put her two cents in on this one.

But not this time. She only looked back at him, thoroughly annoying in her pretended innocence.

He shrugged. "I'll be here a week or two. At least until the baby's born."

"You're a doctor, you said?"

"That's right. I'm in family practice."

"This is…a vacation then?"

"Not really. I'm here to…help Lacey out, in any way I can."

Glances went flying again. He almost wished they would all just say what they were thinking. Then he could answer them. He could explain his position and enlist their aid in convincing Lacey to see things his way.

"Well," said Tess, taking pains to remain neutral. "We hope you'll enjoy your stay."

He was neutral right back at her. "I'm sure I will."

The baby dropped his teething ring. Tess picked it up, wiped it off, and handed it to him, then suggested casually, "We've been trying to talk Lacey into moving to the house."

Lacey reached down the table to brush Tess's arm. "Stop worrying. I told you, I'm just fine at the cabin for right now."

Tess sighed. "I disagree. And I wish Dr. Severance would help me to change your mind."

Fat chance, Logan thought. He said, "I've known Lacey for fifteen years. In all that time, I haven't changed her mind about a single thing."

Lacey laughed. The musical sound tingled along his nerves and warmed something down inside him. "That can't be true, Logan. You must have changed my mind about something in a decade and a half. It's not as if you haven't tried."

He turned his head and looked right at her. The reaction was instantaneous—that chemical thing between them, which unscientific men called desire. It heated his blood, made him glad his lap was covered by Tess Bravo's lace tablecloth.

He should not allow her to do this to him. She was nine months' pregnant, for pity's sake. He ought to be ashamed of himself.

He arched an eyebrow at her. "You're right." To his relief, his voice sounded fine, level and calm. It gave no inkling of what had just happened under the table. "It's incredible when you think about it. But it's true. I have never changed your mind about a single thing."

"Yes. Yes, you have."

"Oh, come on, Lacey."

"I remember distinctly—"

She didn't either, and they both knew she didn't. "What?" he demanded. "You remember what?"

The baby, in his highchair, chortled to himself as a slow smile curved Lacey's eminently kissable mouth. For a moment, Logan thought she would actually say something about the two of them, about how she'd never in her life imagined him as a lover—but that was one thing he had definitely changed her mind about. He had to resist the urge to clap his hand over her mouth.

And then she said, "Broccoli."

He didn't think he'd heard her correctly. "Broccoli?"

Lacey nodded. "You convinced me to give it a try. You said I would like it raw. With ranch dressing."

He stared at her, thinking, Liar. You never ate any broccoli for me—raw or otherwise.

"Yes." That smile of hers was too innocent by half. "Broccoli. Remember?" She was blatantly teasing him, pouring on the innuendo.

But it could be worse, he reminded himself. At least she hadn't said what he'd feared she might.

He forced a smile to answer hers and let her have her silly lie. "I don't know how I could have let myself forget."

"More string beans?" Tess asked him.

He thanked her and spooned a second helping onto his plate.

The talk turned to safer subjects.

Zach asked Jobeth about a calf she had chosen to raise herself as a 4-H project.

Jobeth explained how she planned to experiment with different varieties of feed.

Then Tess wanted to know how things were going for Starr. Evidently, the older girl had a job at a local shop called Cotes's Clothing and Gift.

"A summer job is a summer job," Starr said. "It gets a little boring, but it's not that bad. Mr. Cotes offered me four more hours on Saturdays. I'm going to take them. Might as well make use of my free time this summer. When school starts, I want to keep my focus on studying, where it belongs."

"Our Starr is a straight-A student," Edna declared with pride.

A contrary glint came into the girl's impossibly beautiful violet eyes. "At least I am now."

Zach frowned. "We are proud of you. Very, very proud."

Starr lifted her lovely chin. "Thanks."

Evidently, the girl had had some problems in the past. Logan wondered what, but the subject had already shifted again.

Zach was suggesting that Logan might want to saddle up and ride with him and Jobeth and the men sometime in the next few days. He could see how things were done on a working cattle ranch.

Logan confessed, "I think I've been on a horse about three times in my life. And they weren't very lively horses, if you know what I mean."

Zach chuckled. "We'll find you something sweet-natured and easy-going—or you can ride in one of the pickups. Your choice."

"Then I'd enjoy a tour, Zach. Thanks."

Beside him, Lacey slid back her chair and stood. "Excuse me."

Apprehension pulling a thread of tightness across his chest, Logan looked up over the ripe curve of her belly and into her eyes. "What is it? Are you feeling all right?"

She laughed and put her hand on his shoulder. It felt good there. Damn good. "Relax. I'm fine. I need to… make use of the facilities, that's all."

"You're sure. If something's—"

She lifted her hand and stroked the hair at his temple. "Logan. Eat." Her hand was cool and her eyes were a summer sky—clear, stunningly blue. A smile quivered across that soft mouth of hers. He had to remind himself that they were not alone, or he would have laid his palm on her belly, a possessive touch, which would have felt totally appropriate then. At that moment, she was all softness, all openness. And all for him.

But then she seemed to catch herself. She jerked her glance away. Her smile vanished.

She dropped her hand. "I'll be right back." She slid around the chair and headed for the hall.

He watched her until she'd disappeared from view, reluctant to relinquish the sight of her, wondering at her swift change of mood. For a moment, she had been so damn...tender.

Just as she'd been when he woke and found her standing over him in the cabin an hour before. He'd seen the softness in her eyes then, too. And something else. Worry, maybe.

But softness, definitely.

And even earlier, while he unpacked his few things. She had sat in that rocker and watched him, a dreamy, contented expression on her face.

As if she...

It came to him. Right then, at the Bravo family's dinner table, as he watched her waddle away through the living room, then disappear beyond a door that led to the front hall. It all snapped into place.

For Lacey, this was more than a matter of sexual attraction. More than affection, more than the commonality of a shared past. More even than the most important issue of the child she was about to have.

She was in love with him.

It made perfect sense. The abrupt way she had broken it off in September—that must have been when she had realized.

And what about the times he had called her and she'd never called back? That hadn't been like her. Before, she would have called, if only to insist that she was fine, that he was not to worry about her, that he needed to get on with his life and let her get on with hers.

Yes. She was in love with him—and she feared, because of Jenna, that he would only hurt her.

He wouldn't. Never. Jenna was gone for good now, living in Florida with Mack McGarrity, a baby on the way. She was no threat to what Logan and Lacey might share.

Damn. Lacey loved him.

True, he didn't have a lot of faith in love lately. He'd loved Jenna for all those years and in the end, his love had not been enough to hold her.

But this situation was different. He was already committed to making a life with Lacey. He had been from the moment he'd learned that she carried his child. If Lacey thought herself in love with him—whatever the hell that really meant—it could only work in his favor.

A lightness seemed to move through him. A feeling of rightness, of ease.

And of power, too.

She loved him.

He knew now, with absolute certainty, that she would say yes to him. She had that wild streak. And she was willful. She might not be the wife that Jenna would have been. But she would be his in a way that Jenna never had.

She was already his.

Because she loved him. Lacey Bravo loved him.

He hadn't realized that doubt had been eating at him, eroding his self-confidence, setting his nerves on edge. He hadn't realized it until now, when doubt was gone.

He turned back to the table, a grin pulling at his mouth—and found six pairs of eyes focused on him. Even the baby was watching him.

"That girl's a pistol," Edna muttered under her breath.

"She's independent," said Tess warmly, speaking right up in Lacey's defense. "I admire independence."

Edna gave Tess a fond smile. "Of course you do. So do I. But the fact remains. She needs a husband."

Zach Bravo was still staring at Logan. "You're here to marry her," he said. It wasn't a question.

Logan felt satisfaction, to have it out in the open, to be able to answer simply, "I am."

Zach nodded. "Better not waste any time about it. That baby is likely to show up any minute now."

Chapter 4

It was barely eight-thirty when they got back to the cabin.

Logan suggested that they sit outside for a while and watch the sun set behind the mountains.

Lacey vetoed that idea. "I'm tired," she said.

It was a lie. She wasn't tired. She simply had to get away from him. Having him so near, having to be so very careful, was making her crazy.

She was no good at carefulness. She had never taught herself how to hide what was in her heart. She wore her emotions on the surface. And she liked it that way, felt comfortable in her own skin because she could always be honest about what was going on inside her. And it translated into her work, gave her a freedom to create whatever came to her, to follow her own ideas wherever they wanted to take her.

But she couldn't afford to let her emotions show now. If she did, Logan would only use her poor heart against her. Her love would become his ally in his relentless quest to do the right thing—the Logan Severance version of the right thing, which included marrying the mother of his child whether he loved her or not.

She had to watch herself every minute. And still, she kept messing up, kept slipping into ridiculous moments of pure adoration. Kept snapping to attention to find herself staring at him dreamy-eyed, mooning over him as he slept, caressing the side of his face at the dinner table while Zach and his family looked on.

He was watching her strangely now, one corner of that sexy mouth tipped up, a musing, thoroughly nerve-racking look in his eyes. "Tired? You? The original night owl?"

He had her dead to rights, of course. Even far advanced in pregnancy, Lacey Bravo *was* a night owl. She went to bed late and if she got up by noon, she felt she'd started the day good and early.

She stuck with her lie. "Tonight, I *am* tired. I'm taking a shower and I'm going to bed."

Of course, once she got there, she knew she wasn't going to be able to sleep.

She decided to do a few exercises. She practiced her Kegels—contracting and relaxing the muscles she would use in childbirth. She sat up and rolled her neck and did a few simple stretches. She got on her hands and knees and flexed her back, then relaxed it, remaining aware of her breathing the whole time.

When she ran out of exercises, she tried to concentrate on a novel, sitting up among the pillows, the book propped on her big stomach. But her attention wandered. The baby seemed restless. The little sweetheart kept surprising her with nudges and pokes. And her back was aching. It was hard to get comfortable.

She heard Logan go out to the bathroom, heard the water pipes sighing as he took his shower. When he came back in, she heard him moving around in the main room and wondered just what he was doing out there.

Then she heard the click as he turned off the light over the table. The springs of the daybed creaked. And then silence.

From outside, faintly, came the far-off howling of lonely coyotes and the hooting of an owl. But there was no sound at all from the main room. She continued her attempt at reading until ten, then gave up and turned off her own light.

As the hours crawled by and she couldn't sleep, she silently called Logan Severance a hundred nasty names. She practiced more Kegels—hundreds of them. She sat up and rolled her neck, stretched her arms, closed her eyes, breathed slowly and evenly in and out, seeking relaxation and inner peace.

Hah.

By midnight, her poor bladder could no longer be denied. She pulled on her robe and tiptoed out to the back door. With agonizing care, she turned the latch, then tried to pull the door open slowly enough that the old hinges wouldn't creak.

They didn't. Or if they did, it was just barely.

Still, he heard them. "Lacey?" His voice was thick with the groggy remnants of sleep.

If she hadn't loved him so blasted much, she could have hated him for that, for his ability to drop right off to sleep while she lay staring wide-eyed into the shadows, counting her Kegels—not to mention the seconds, the minutes, the *hours.*

He sat up. She could see the shape of him, outlined in the moonlight that streamed in, pale and silvery, through the window above the daybed. "What's wrong?"

"Nothing." She pushed the door open the rest of the way and lumbered out into the night.

When she came back, the light was on and he was standing by the rocker, wearing a pair of navy blue sweats and nothing else that she could detect. He had his bare arms folded over his chest.

"Are you in labor?"

She let loose an unladylike grunt. "Is that an accusation?"

He dropped his arms. Lord, that chest of his was beautiful. Planes and angles, power and the readiness for motion. Da Vinci would have drooled. "Come on, Lace. Are you having contractions? That's all I want to know."

"No." She gathered her robe closer around the barrel of her belly. "I am not having contractions. And honestly, there is no need to ask me that. I can assure you, when I *am* in labor, I will have no hesitation at all about sharing the news with you."

"Believe it or not, sometimes a woman won't even know when she's in labor." He was grinning.

"You know, Doctor. You are way too cheerful about all of this."

"It just occurred to me. You haven't called me Dr. Do-Right once since I arrived here."

"I guess I must be slipping—and I'm sure you mean, a woman might not know when she's in the *early stages* of labor. After a certain point, it's got to become pretty obvious."

"True." He frowned. "Did you ever get a chance to take a childbirth class?"

"No. But I bought a few books and I've been studying them, getting to…understand what will happen."

"Well. Good." There it was again—that musing look in his eye, that half-smile on his lips.

"What is that?"

He lifted a dark brow. "What?"

"That…look."

"Look?"

"Yes, Logan. That look. That look that says you know something I don't."

He lifted both big, sculpted shoulders. "Beats me."

She wanted to slug him. Or kiss him. She said, "I'm going back to bed. And if I get up again, could you pretend not to notice? It's bad enough that I spend my nights going in and out of the back door. I don't need you hovering nearby ready to check my vital signs every time I come in."

"Will do."

"What does that mean?"

"Unless you call for me, I won't get up."

"Thank you."

"You are very welcome."

She peered at him. "What is going on?"

"Nothing. Go on back to bed."

It was good advice, and she knew it. She ducked into the sleeping nook, dragged her poor ungainly body onto the bed and curled on her side. The light in the main room went out.

The next time she got up, about two hours later, Logan didn't even stir.

Daylight came as it always did: earlier than Lacey would have liked.

Not that she noticed. By then, as always, she was finally sound asleep. If Logan went outside, she didn't hear it, and she didn't hear him come back in, either.

But she did hear him fiddling with the stove.

She turned over and grumbled to herself and drifted back into a pleasant, floating state of slumber, thinking as sleep claimed her that at least he was trying to be quiet.

Not much later, she found herself awake again. She sighed, breathed deeply, told herself to relax and let go.

But there was a problem.

She could swear she heard every move he made. The clink of a bowl as he set it on the table, the rustle of cereal spilling out of a box. The muffled click— twice—as he carefully opened, then closed the refrigerator door, the pad of his stocking feet across the plank floor, the glug-glug-glug of milk poured from a carton.

She tried putting her pillow over her head, then even yanked the blankets over that. It did no good.

She was awake—at eight thirty-three in the morning, after having slept fewer than four measly hours.

She knew that Logan usually woke around six. Which meant that in all likelihood, he'd been lying there for at least a couple of hours, actively restraining himself from getting up and starting in with his annoying morning-person activities. The only reason he would do such a thing was to give her a chance to sleep undisturbed.

It was thoughtful of him. And she should have been grateful.

But she wasn't grateful.

She was nine months pregnant and she was tired and Logan Severance was driving her crazy with his will of iron and his musing I-know-something-you-don't-know smiles and his absolute refusal to accept that she was never, ever going to say "I do."

Lacey pulled the pillow closer around her face and muttered a few choice naughty words.

Couldn't he see that it would never work? Even if he returned her love, what possible chance did they have of making it as a couple? They didn't even get up at the same time.

He went back to the refrigerator—did he actually imagine she couldn't hear every move he made?—and put the milk away. Then back to the table again. He didn't scrape the floor with the chair, but it creaked when he sat down. His spoon clinked against the bowl.

When she found herself straining to hear him chew, she knew it was no use.

With another low oath, she shoved back the covers and reached for the tent of the day, a scoop-necked, ankle-length, teal-blue creation, which she'd left hanging on a wall peg along with her bra the night before. Her ballerina flats were right there, too, in the tiny space to the right of the bed. She tore off her sleep shirt and put on the clothes, shivering a little with cold, realizing that he must not have built a fire after all, even though she'd distinctly heard him fooling around with the stove.

When she entered the main room, he looked up in mid-crunch. She didn't say a word, just went out the door and into the bathroom, where she relieved her overworked bladder and splashed icy water on her face and grumbled to herself in the mirror as she raked a brush through her hair.

Logan was over at the stove, clattering the iron covers, when she reentered the cabin. He sent a smile over his shoulder. "Now you're up, I'll make a fire."

He rumpled a newspaper and fed it into the belly of the stove as she went to the old electric percolator on the counter by the sink, filled it with water and plugged it in.

"You're drinking coffee?" A frown of doctorly concern creased his brow.

She unplugged the pot, took the lid off and tipped it so that he could see inside. "Just water. I'm heating water. For tea. *Herbal* tea. Does that meet with your approval?"

"Yes," he said gently. "As a matter of fact, it does." He turned back to the stove. She took a tea bag from the canister and dropped it into a mug. Then, since it never took the water that long to boil, she just stood there at the counter, waiting for it.

"Are you hungry?" he asked, once he'd lit the fire and was carefully putting the cover back in place.

"I'll get myself some cereal."

"Are you sure? Maybe an egg——"

She looked at him. The look must have said exactly what she was thinking.

"Not an egg person, huh?"

"Not in the last, oh, eight months or so."

"I understand."

She doubted it, but she decided not to comment. Soon enough, the water was hot. "There's some instant coffee, if you want it," she muttered grudgingly as she poured the boiling water over her tea bag.

"No, thanks. The cereal's fine."

She carried a bowl and spoon to the table with her. The cereal was already there. He went to the refrigerator and got her the milk. Soon enough, they were sitting across the table from each other, crunching away.

Lacey tried to concentrate on her cereal. She took slow bites and she chewed thoroughly. She'd discovered, especially over the past month, when her entire digestive system seemed to have been crammed into a tiny space between her swollen uterus and her lungs, that if she didn't eat slowly, either hiccups or heartburn would be the result.

"I tried not to wake you," he said with regret, after a few moments of mutual chewing and swallowing.

She sent him a glance. "But you did."

"You're angry."

"No." She had to chew some more. He waited. Once she'd swallowed, she told him, "I was angry when you woke me up. Now I'm…" She sought the word. It came to her. "…philosophical."

He set down his spoon. He looked much too amused. "You? Philosophical?"

She scooped up more cereal, poked it into her mouth. "Uh-huh."

He watched her as she chewed. When she swallowed, he said, "I assume you intend to elaborate."

As a matter of fact, she did. She nodded. "It's just come to me. In a blinding flash of insight."

He muttered, "I'll bet."

"I mean it." She left her spoon in her bowl, braced her elbow on the table and leaned her chin on her hand. "It has. It really has."

"All right. I'll bite. What has come to you?"

Her stomach felt squashed. She arched her back, rubbed at the base of her spine, then settled into her earlier pose, chin in hand. "Our basic natures are at odds."

"Meaning?"

"The fact that you love my sister aside, there really is no hope for us—as a couple, I mean."

His jaw twitched. "That's your opinion."

She sighed. "Remember that old story—the ant and the grasshopper?"

He dared to groan. "You're kidding."

"Nope. You're the ant. Up at first light. Diligent and hardworking, upwardly mobile, always getting ready for a rainy day."

"I'm an ant." He did not look pleased.

She gave him a lazy grin. "That's right. I, on the other hand, am all grasshopper." She gestured at the small, dim room around them. "I take everything— each day—as it comes. I live for the joy of the moment. You don't understand me and I don't understand you.

We're just…much too different by nature to have a prayer of making a go of it together."

He studied her for a long moment, looking irritatingly amused. "Correct me if I'm wrong, but as I recall the story, when winter came, the grasshopper died."

She hit the table with the heel of her hand. "See? Total ant logic. Focusing on the very things you can least control."

"I assume you mean death."

"Yes. Exactly. Death. And bad weather, too." She picked up her spoon again and went back to work on the cereal.

"I thought that was the moral of the story," Logan said. "The ant worked hard and scrimped and saved and lasted the winter. The grasshopper partied. And when the cold weather came…" He shook his head and pretended to look mournful. "Too bad, so sad."

She pointed her spoon at him. "I live in L.A. Bad weather is not a problem."

"We're discussing a fable, Lace. In a fable, bad weather stands for any of a number of possible difficult periods in life."

She'd started out this little discussion feeling pleasantly superior—now she felt just plain disgruntled. "Oh, never mind. You're determined to miss my point and make your own."

"I got your point."

"Right." She bent her head over her bowl and finished her cereal, aware of his eyes on her the whole time.

When she looked up, sure enough, he was watching her.

He said, "Maybe having my baby is the best thing that ever happened to you. As my wife, you know you'll always have a roof over your head when winter closes in."

She reached for the bottle of prenatal vitamins in the center of the table, screwed off the lid and shook one into her hand. "Listen to me, Logan. I'm not going to be your wife. And as far as that roof you mentioned, I don't *need* to know it'll be there. I don't think that far ahead. As I keep trying to explain to you, I'm a grasshopper to the core."

"Fine. So I'll think ahead for you. You *do* need that. Especially now, with the baby coming."

She picked up her bowl and stood. "I can see I'm getting nowhere."

"I wouldn't say that. This has been an enlightening discussion."

"Enlightening for you, maybe."

There it was again, that musing, knowing look in his eyes. "Seriously. I think we have a lot to offer each other."

"Dream on."

"I'll scrimp and save for a rainy day. You'll see that we make the most of every moment. We're the perfect couple."

Something scathing rose to her lips. She bit it back and turned for the sink, where she washed her vitamin down with water, cleaned her bowl and spoon and set them in the wooden rack to dry.

"He seems a fine man," Tess said. "And so handsome, too."

They were sitting in a pair of rockers on the porch

of the main house, just Tess and Lacey, enjoying the shade in the heat of the afternoon. Zach and Jobeth had taken Logan out for a look around the ranch, Starr had driven off that morning to her summer job and Edna had settled in with the baby at her own house for a short nap.

"Lacey, did you hear what I said?"

Lacey made a noncommittal sound. She had her sketch pad perched on what was left of her lap and she was busy stroking in shadows with the side of her pencil.

Tess took a few more tiny, perfect stitches on the thick wool sock she was darning. "I hope he got everything worked out all right with the other doctors at his office."

Logan had tried calling his office via cell phone earlier. When the cell phone cut out on him, he'd ended up using the phone at the main house.

"Yes," Lacey said. "His partners have agreed to cover for him."

"Well. That's good."

Was it? Lacey wasn't so sure. But she felt no urge to remark on the fact. She focused on her drawing, her hand moving swiftly and surely over the paper.

Tess cleared her throat. "Maybe I have no right to ask, but I'm going to ask anyway…"

Lacey made a series of quick, deft strokes, crosshatching more shadows, then looked up from her sketch pad. "Yes," she said, "Logan is the baby's father."

Those big dark eyes of Tess's didn't waver. "He says he's here to marry you."

"When did he say that?"

"Last night. You had left the table for a moment."
Tess snipped with her scissors and tied off her thread.
"Will you marry him?"

"No." Lacey flipped the cover over her drawing and
set the pad on the short bench between them.

"Why not?"

Lacey's back was aching, as it had been for the past
few days. She pushed herself from the chair and in-
dulged in a nice, protracted stretch. Tess watched her,
saying nothing.

Lacey wandered to the railing and managed to hoist
herself up onto it. She put one hand under her belly to
support it a little and leaned her cheek against the porch
post.

Then she said it. "He doesn't love me. He's always
loved Jenna."

Tess bent to her basket, dropped in the sock, and
brought out a plaid shirt with a tear at the shoulder
seam. "How do you know that?"

"They were high school sweethearts. And they were
even engaged, last year, before Mack McGarrity came
back into the picture."

"That was last year. What about now?"

"I've...confronted him with it. Yesterday, when he
first arrived and started insisting that we had to get
married."

"And?"

"He didn't come right out and say, 'I love Jenna,' but
he never denied it, either."

Tess looked over the rows of thread spools in her
sewing box, seeking the right color. "Your sister is no

threat to your relationship with Logan. Jenna loves her husband."

"Unfortunately, that hasn't stopped Logan from loving *her*."

"Or so you assume, though he's never actually said as much."

"He doesn't have to say it. I know. And he certainly hasn't said he loves me."

"Have you said you love him?"

"No, and I don't intend to."

"Why not?"

Lacey considered that question—and decided against answering it. Tess didn't seem to mind. She got to work threading her needle, rolling a knot into the end of the thread. She took her first stitch.

Her head still bent over her mending, Tess spoke again. "Whatever Dr. Severance feels for your sister, it's obvious he cares for you. And he also feels...what a man feels when he looks at a certain woman."

Lacey sat a little straighter on the railing. "Sex, you mean?"

"Yes. I mean sex."

"Oh, come on. He did...want me. Nine months ago. But now..."

"He wants you," said Tess patiently. "And I am not talking about nine months ago. I am talking about what I saw on his face last night."

"You imagined it."

"No, I didn't." Tess glanced up in mid-stitch. "And you *do* love *him*."

Lacey considered a lie of denial and rejected the idea. Tess would know a lie when she heard one. Lacey looked out, over the yard, past the silvery foliage of the Russian olive tree growing in the center of the driveway, to the rolling green land that would soon parch to gold beneath the summer sun. "I'm not going to marry him." She said it very softly.

"Excuse me?"

Lacey turned back to the shade of the porch. A fly buzzed near her ear. She waved it away. "I said, I'm not going to marry him."

Tess kept her gaze on her mending, but a smile curved her mouth. "He's a fine man. And he cares for you. He wants you as a man wants a woman. And you love him. It's enough."

"Enough for what?"

"Enough for a start. Enough to build on. That's all that's really needed at the first in a marriage, if the two people are honorable. If they're willing to persist."

Lacey peered more closely at her cousin's wife. "You sound as though you're talking from experience."

"I am. Zach and I started out with a strictly practical arrangement. He needed a wife. And I needed…a place like this ranch. Somewhere to call home."

Lacey let out a short laugh of pure disbelief. "You and Zach? You're kidding. I can see when he looks at you how he feels. And when you look at him…"

A sweet pink blush crept upward over Tess's soft cheeks. "Yes. But it wasn't always that way."

Bracing her hand more firmly beneath her heavy stomach, Lacey lowered her feet to the porch boards. "Well. Call me a fool. Call me a romantic. But I want to have my husband's love when I marry him."

"Ah, but not just *any* husband. You want Logan Severance's love."

Right then, as if the forces of nature had some vested interest in proving Tess's point, a gust of wind blew down the porch. It ruffled back the cover on Lacey's sketch pad. The drawing Lacey had just been working on—of Logan napping in the cabin—was right there for Tess to see. She glanced at it.

"Very nice," she said.

Lacey stepped forward, flipped the cover in place and turned the pad over so the cardboard backing would hold it shut. "All right. So it's Logan's love I want. So what? Sometimes people can't have what they want."

"That's true. And they certainly will never get what they want if they don't even try."

"And just how do you suggest that I 'try'?"

Tess took a few more perfect stitches, her head tipped thoughtfully to the side. When she pulled the thread through for the third time, she spoke. "Marry him. Build a life with him. Raise that baby together. Give love a place to grow."

Give love a place to grow. What a captivating idea. Too captivating. "That might work for some couples. But not for Logan and me. There are just a hundred ways we don't mesh."

"And those ways are?"

"Well, for starters, at least with me, he can be unbelievably overbearing."

"And you're a born rebel. Your lives will never be dull."

"You don't understand, Tess. You don't know. He is

a fine man, just as you said. But I'm not…wife material. Not the kind of wife Logan's always wanted, anyway."

"You will be an excellent wife. You're strong and good-hearted and full of life. Logan Severance is a lucky man to have your love."

Lacey shook her head. "Tess, you're not listening. It simply can't work."

"Shall I tell you what my wise old Aunt Matilda used to say?"

"I'll pass."

Tess chuckled. "Listen up."

"Oh, all right. Go ahead."

"Whether you think you can or you think you *can't*—you're right."

Logan, Zach and Jobeth returned about half an hour later. Tess went in and brought out a pitcher of lemonade and five tall iced glasses. For a while, they all sat together on the porch. Logan asked questions about what he'd seen on his afternoon tour and Zach answered him in that low, pleasant drawl of his.

Lacey sat in the rocker, sipping lemonade and sometimes sketching, listening to the others talk. Now and then Logan would glance her way. Their eyes would meet and she'd find herself thinking about what Tess had said.

Marry him. Raise that baby together. Give love a place to grow….

Somehow, right then, in the shade of her cousin's porch on a hot summer afternoon, Tess's lovely, impossible words sounded like excellent advice. Lacey felt good, lazy and content and happy with the world and her own rather insecure place in it.

Even the ache in her back wasn't that bad, though sometimes it did seem to reach around, feeling like thin yet powerful fingers, and squeeze at her distended abdomen. She wondered, as she sat there idly rocking, if she might be having contractions—and then decided that if she was, there was nothing urgent about them. They came irregularly and were never less than ten or fifteen minutes apart.

Edna strolled across the yard with the baby at a little after five and Starr came spinning down the driveway in a dusty sports car a few minutes later.

Tess picked up her mending and her cloth-covered sewing box and stood. "I think it's time I started thinking about getting some food on the table. Lacey? Logan? I hope you'll join us."

"Yes," said Edna. "Please stay. There is plenty."

So they stayed. They walked back to the cabin together at twilight. Logan insisted on carrying her big shoulder tote, which Lacey took everywhere so she'd always have her sketch pads and pencils with her if she needed them.

He reached for her hand halfway down the dirt road and she gave it to him. In fact, she wrapped the fingers of her other hand around his arm and leaned in close. He felt so solid and good, someone she could always lean against and know that he could take the weight.

She chuckled to herself.

He turned, smiled. "What?"

"I was just thinking that you're great for leaning on."

She regretted the words as soon as they were out of

her mouth, certain that he would consider them nothing short of an invitation to start in about marriage again.

But he surprised her. He only squeezed her hand, murmured, "Lean all you want," and kept walking.

When they got to the cabin, he made the same suggestion he had the night before, that they sit outside for a while. And this time she accepted his invitation.

They sat on the step and listened to the coyotes howl at the risen moon and hardly talked at all. Talking didn't seem necessary, somehow.

When they went in, Lacey showered first, standing under the arching shower pipe that had been added on to the claw-footed tub. As the water cascaded over her swollen body, it occurred to her that never once since breakfast had he used the dreaded "M" word.

Was that progress?

She didn't know. And she didn't really even care. The day had been a good one, all in all. And she *was* a born grasshopper, someone who knew how to take each day as it came.

She was in bed by ten, listening to Logan's movements in the main part of the cabin, practicing her pregnant-lady exercises, and wishing that the pain in her back would go away. She felt a little keyed up, and her legs were cramping just a bit. She expected another mostly sleepless night.

But surprisingly, she dropped off around eleven.

She woke at one in the morning. She sat straight up in bed as a powerful contraction gripped her. She groaned, a loud, animal sound, one she couldn't have held back if she'd tried.

The light went on in the main room.

Lacey hardly noticed. The contraction lasted forever, a vise of pressure, gripping, holding, not letting go. She went on groaning and tried to breathe, to relax, to go with the pain.

"Lace?"

A strong hand pushed back the curtain to the main room. Lacey found herself staring into Logan's midnight eyes.

He didn't speak. She was grateful for that. She closed her eyes and moaned some more until the contraction finally loosed its grip on her.

Then she realized that the bed was wet. She pushed back the covers. The sweet smell of amniotic fluid drifted up to her nostrils.

She met Logan's eyes again. "The baby's coming," she said. "The baby's coming right now."

Chapter 5

Logan was so calm.

He led her out to the bathroom and gently took away her sodden sleep shirt. She had another contraction right then, standing there naked on the bathroom rug. She sank to her knees.

Logan knelt beside her and gave her his hand. She gripped it as hard as she could while he whispered to her, "Relax, now. Breathe…and relax…"

She let out another of those animal groans. "I have to push, Logan. I have to—"

"No. Don't push. We need to see what's really going on first. Don't push yet. Pant. Come on, short, fast breaths."

She panted. "It was only…" Another groan escaped. "Only two or three minutes, since the last one…"

"It's all right. Everything's fine. Everything's all right."

She panted. She groaned. Great, deep, rumbling, animal groans. When finally the huge invisible hands on her belly relaxed a little, Logan said very gently, "Come on. Let's rinse you off. You'll feel better…"

There were two sets of taps in the old claw-footed tub, one to the tub itself and another for the shower. He turned on the lower ones and helped her climb in over the tub's high, curved sides. She shot him a look of alarm as she noted the red streaks on the inside of her thighs. "There's some blood…"

"It's only bloody show. Perfectly normal. I saw it in the bed, too. But no meconium staining that I can see." He tested the water. "Damn. Still cold. Wait just a minute, sweetheart."

Sweetheart. Even now, naked and huge in front of the man she loved, sweating and confused and expecting the next unbearable contraction to descend any second now, *sweetheart* sounded so good.

"Meconium?" Her befuddled mind tried to place the word.

"Greenish-brown fluid. From the baby's digestive tract. It can sometimes indicate fetal distress."

"But there isn't any, right?"

"No. No meconium. And that's good." He tested the water again. "Okay. The water's running warm enough. Come on." They cupped water in their hands and splashed it over her, together rinsing the sticky fluid from her belly and her thighs.

Then Logan said, "I think we should use soap, just in case…"

She stared at him and it hit her all over again. Her baby was coming and it was coming fast.

She picked up the soap and washed herself thoroughly. Logan soaped his hands as well. Then together, they splashed on more water, rinsing her clean—and it happened again. Another contraction. She squatted right there in the tub, threw back her head and howled.

It lasted a lifetime, but when it finally eased a little and she came back to herself, Logan had found the rubbing alcohol and was dousing his hands with it. He rinsed again and gave her a reassuring smile. "Lie back. Let's have a look…"

He examined her, right there in the tub. And when he was done, he asked, "How far is the hospital?"

"Uh…I don't know. Twenty miles or so."

He swore, but very gently.

"What?"

"I'm not sure you can make it."

"Oh, Logan…" She wanted to be braver, but it was a cry of distress.

"Listen." His voice was a soothing caress. "Everything is normal. The baby's in the right position. You are completely effaced. And you are fully dilated. Do you know what that means?"

"Ready to push, right? But how is that possible?"

"When it comes to having babies, almost anything is possible. And I don't think it's a good idea to ask you to try and hold back for the time it will take to get you to the hospital." He picked up the soap again and began scrubbing his hands for the second time. "You might succeed, but you could slow things down and only make it more difficult in the end. Or you might *not* succeed. And you'd end up having the baby on the side of the road. It's better, I think, if we stay here—at least till help arrives."

She'd been sweating a moment ago, now she was shivering all of a sudden, shaking all over.

Logan grabbed a towel, dried his hands and turned on the space heater in the corner by the door. Then he came back and began pulling towels off the shelf. He knelt, wrapped them around her, and rubbed at her shoulders to get the circulation going. "Better?"

"A little."

"Where's the phone number for your doctor—and the one for the main house?"

She told him.

He turned for the door.

Absolute terror gripped her. "Oh, God. Logan. Don't go…"

"I'll be right back. It won't be three minutes, I swear to you. And maybe I'll get lucky and get through on the cell phone."

She bit her lip and tasted blood—but she kept her mouth shut when he left her.

A minute passed. She knew because she counted the seconds. And then she didn't count anymore because the next contraction claimed her. She rose onto her haunches, grabbed the sides of the tub again and rode it as it crested and finally waned.

Then Logan was kneeling beside her, wrapping a blanket around her. "I got through. They're sending an ambulance. Forty-five minutes tops, they said. And Tess will be here in ten with the things we're going to need." He bent over her. "Do you want to get out of the tub?"

She stared at his lips, wondering why he was asking her that. "I don't…"

He smiled at her reassuringly and stroked the side of her face. His hand felt so good, so solid, warm and real. "This is a pretty big tub. You could just stay here, if you want, until Tess arrives with the things to get the bed ready."

She shivered some more, but not as badly as before. The little room was getting warmer. "I'd like…to walk for a bit."

"Sounds good." He helped her from the tub.

Lacey clutched the blanket around her and they trudged back and forth in the short space between the tub and the door—until another contraction doubled her over.

Logan went down to the floor with her again. He whispered to her to breathe, not to push yet, just to wait a little while. She groaned and tried to do what he said, to hold back. At the same time, she wanted to shove him away, to shout at him that she was the one doing this and she'd push if she wanted to.

By the time the contraction passed, she was sweating again. She threw off the blanket and asked for a clean sleep shirt.

"Where?"

"Top bureau drawer."

He left her for the second time. She didn't mind as much as before. Some change had come over her. Some strange, calm feeling. She would do this. She would get through this. She—and her baby—would be fine.

"Tess is here," Logan said when he came back. Lacey was kneeling on the rug again then, her forehead against the rim of the sink basin. The only response she could give him right then was a groan.

He waited for the contraction to ease, then helped her up. "Here." He settled the shirt over her head and she put her arms through the sleeves. "Tess is getting the bed ready and making the fire."

"Don't need...the fire. I'm sweating. Can't you see?"

He smiled and got a washcloth and wet it with cool water.

She sighed when he wiped her face with it. "Heaven..."

Or it was, for a few too-brief moments. Then another contraction struck. She got through it, and then two more after that, relaxing into them as if they were waves—waves that rolled in, rolled through her, then rolled away. They didn't seem to hurt so much as before, though in a way they felt stronger, more focused, more purposeful, somehow.

Finally, Tess stuck her head in the bathroom door. "All ready."

"Then let's go," Logan said.

They went into the cabin, where Tess had removed the curtain that separated the sleeping nook from the rest of the room. The bed had only a white sheet on it, and a number of pillows. There was a stack of towels and one of the receiving blankets on the edge of the bed and a basin of water on a chair.

When Lacey crawled onto the bed, the sheet crackled. Tess had thought to put plastic—a tablecloth or a shower curtain, probably—between the mattress and the sheet. She helped Lacey to arrange the pillows against the headboard, so she could lie in a semi-sitting position, as Logan went to wash his hands again.

"Thirsty?" Tess smiled at her.

Lacey nodded. Tess had a full pitcher of water right by the bed. She filled a glass and Lacey sipped. Then Logan came back and examined her again.

She looked at his dark head between her spread thighs and couldn't help remarking, "I feel so utterly demure."

He glanced up and winked at her. "Always have been."

She thought, I have never loved you so much as I do at this moment.

"Ready to push," he said.

Lacey grunted. "This is news?"

He and Tess both chuckled, but Lacey hardly noticed. She felt the contraction coming. And she wrapped her hands around her thighs and bore down.

"Do what you feel," Logan said softly. "Bear down until you can't hold your breath any longer. Then take in another one…and bear down again. Let it go, let it happen."

She let out a loud moan. "Logan, I can do this. Just let me…"

He said something gentle in reply. But she didn't really hear it. She had a job to do and, miraculously, she knew how to do it. She sucked in a giant breath and bore down, groaning without shame. When she ran out of breath, she sucked in more and bore down again.

She felt strong, and sure. It wasn't that bad. It wasn't bad at all. And between contractions, she actually rested, with Logan and Tess attending her, letting her wet her lips with cool water, rubbing her back and neck when she would allow that, pressing damp cloths to her sweating brow and the back of her neck.

When the contractions came, she heard them talking, heard it when Tess cried, "There it is. The baby's head. I can see it."

But Tess—and Logan, too—seemed far away to her. The world to her was the hard fist of her contractions, the rising of her uterus and then the bearing down.

"Scoot down now," Logan said, during one of the blessed moments when her body allowed her to rest.

They had put a pair of chairs at the end of the bed. Lacey moved down to them. Logan instructed her to brace her feet, one on each chair. Tess set a basin between the chairs and tucked pillows at Lacey's back and shoulders to help her stay in the most effective position to push the baby out.

When the next contraction hit, Logan said, "This is it. Easy. Pant. Blow. Don't push too hard…"

Lacey made a deep, growling sound. The pressure became almost unbearably intense as her body gave to let the head emerge. Tess said, "Oh!" in a voice full of wonder.

Logan had his hands down there, applying a gentle counter-pressure. "Slow," he said, "careful, not too fast…"

Seconds later, the intense pressure eased.

"The head is out," Logan said.

Lacey looked down at the red, smashed-looking thing between her legs. "Oh, dear Lord. Is it all right?"

"It's fine," Logan said. "The baby's fine. And you

are fine. We have no tearing. No tearing at all." His hands worked at the sides of the squashed nose and downward, gently stroking, over the tiny, ugly chin, and the wrinkled throat. Fluid dribbled from the baby's mouth and nose.

"There," Logan said.

"There what?" Lacey demanded.

"That should clear out any mucus that might be obstructing the airways. Now we're ready to let those shoulders out. Are you ready to push again?"

Lacey panted and nodded.

He cradled the baby's head, oh so gently, in his two strong hands. "Okay, push now, push…" She pushed and he lifted the head. "There," he said, "Yes. The lower shoulder is free…"

After that, it was over in less than a minute. Baby and fluids gushed out in a rush. She heard a cry—her baby's cry.

"It's a girl," Logan said. "A beautiful, little girl."

Logan didn't cut the umbilical cord. He said he would leave that for the EMTs, who would have the proper equipment. He wiped most of the blood and fluids from the body of the squirming baby, examining her as he did it, and then pronounced her "a perfect ten."

Tess helped Lacey to scoot back up onto the bed, where she could rest, at last, fully on her back. Lacey pulled up her sleep shirt and Logan gave her the ugly, wonderful baby to lay on her bare breast.

Lacey looked down at the tiny, whining creature with the slightly pointy head, still connected to her body by the pulsing cord, and knew that her life was unutterably changed.

Logan was bending over them both.

And Tess had made herself scarce, somewhere over by the sink.

Lacey spent a moment touching her baby, whispering to her, stroking her warm, mottled skin. Then from the little one, she reached up and touched the side of Logan's face.

At her breast, her baby rooted fitfully. Lacey tried to help her find the nipple, but she didn't quite manage to latch on and stay there.

"She'll learn," Logan said.

"I want to call her Margaret," Lacey told him. "For my mother." She laughed, and then groaned a little, as a mild contraction squeezed her tired abdomen. "My mother was a wonderful woman. And I know that for a few years there, I made her life a living hell. Maybe she'll look down from heaven and see this little angel and be glad she had me, after all."

"I think she's glad," Logan said. "In fact, I know it." Then he murmured, "Margaret," in a musing tone. He nodded. "I like it."

"And *your* mother…?" she asked. "What was her name?" Logan's mother had died when he was six months old. His father, lost to a first heart attack about five years ago, had raised him alone.

"Rose," Logan said. "Her name was Rose."

Lacey stroked her baby's slightly sticky head. "Margaret Rose, then. What do you think?"

She had never seen his eyes look so soft—or so very dark. "Yes," he said. "All right. Margaret Rose."

"Rosie, for short."

"Rosie it is." He put down his index finger. It brushed Lacey's bare breast and then Rosie's wrinkled red fist. Tiny perfect fingers opened—and closed, holding on.

"She's strong," Logan said in a voice low with emotion. "Strong and healthy. Lace, you did a hell of a job."

"Praise? From you—directed at me? Are you feeling all right?"

"I don't think I've ever felt better in my life."

The words were there, in her heart, rising up, undeniable.

She didn't know why she'd ever cared to deny them. Why she'd ever thought it wise to hide the truth from him.

All her old fears and hesitations, her need to guard her independence and protect her woman's pride, seemed foolish now. She didn't need to deny her love anymore, not after what she'd just been through—what all three of them had been through: she and Logan and this tiny miracle who lay rooting at her breast, clutching Logan's index finger, making soft, mewling sounds.

"I love you, Logan," she whispered.

His eyes grew softer still. He started to speak. She put her hand to his lips. "Shh. It's okay. It's just... I wanted you to know. I've known for nine months. It's been my big secret. But it seems kind of silly now, after this, to go on keeping it. It seems like the best thing just to let you know."

He nodded, and pressed his lips to her temple. They

sighed together and their daughter gave a small, impatient cry.

A few minutes later, the ambulance pulled up in the yard.

Chapter 6

Dr. Pruitt arrived with the ambulance. He clamped and cut the umbilical cord. Then he supervised as Lacey pushed out the afterbirth. He performed a formal post-natal exam and weighed the baby: seven pounds, two ounces. He also examined Lacey.

When he was done, he confirmed what everyone already knew: mother and daughter were doing just fine. He said he saw no need for a hospital visit, especially when he learned that the baby's father was a doctor and would be in close attendance over the next twenty-four hours.

The ambulance drove away less than an hour after it had arrived, at a little after three in the morning. Tess suggested a move to the main house, but Lacey vetoed that. She had Logan to look after her and Rosie. And the little cabin somehow seemed like home now. She wanted to stay there, for the next few days at least, just the three of them.

And then…well, she'd worry about that when the time came.

Tess called Zach on the cell phone and instructed him to pile all the baby equipment into the pickup and bring it on over.

"We're keeping everyone awake tonight," Lacey said ruefully, after Tess had hung up.

Tess waved a hand. "We are ranchers," she said. "We're used to being up all hours of the night."

Lacey and Logan took Rosie to the bathroom. Logan held the baby while Lacey showered and changed into a nightgown that buttoned down the front. Then Lacey rested, sitting on the rug with the commode to lean against, as Logan gave Rosie her first bath—which amounted to a few gentle strokes with a warm wash-cloth.

When they got back to the main room, Tess had changed the sheets again and put up the curtain that made the sleeping nook into its own private space. Lacey climbed gratefully onto the bed and drank two glasses of cool water as Logan, over at the daybed, put on Rosie's first diaper. Tess helped Lacey to get comfortable. Then Logan laid their daughter beside her. The baby rooted at her breast. This time, the little darling actually managed to latch on.

"Let her nurse for five minutes or so on that side," Tess said. "They we'll try the other one."

By the time Logan and Tess tiptoed out, Lacey was as deep in sleep as Rosie. She didn't even hear them bring in all the baby things.

* * *

Lacey woke when Rosie did, about three hours after she'd fallen asleep.

She looked down at the fuzzy, misshapen little head of her daughter and groused, "You aren't going to turn out to be a day person like your father, are you?"

Rosie opened her tiny mouth—first for a big yawn, and right after that, to let out a wail.

The curtain slid back and Logan was there, looking tired and rumpled and absolutely wonderful. "Good morning."

Lacey gave him a smile with all of her newly revealed love in it. "This baby is hungry."

"That's the way babies are. What about you?"

"I'm starved. But I think she's going to insist on eating first. Let's try it in the rocker this time."

It was quite an experience, getting out of that bed. Lacey's body felt as if she'd done something horrible to it—like go through childbirth. Her uterus was still cramping, everything lower down ached from all that pushing—and the last thing she ever wanted to do again was to stand up straight.

Logan chuckled. "I hope you don't feel as bad as you look."

She moaned and muttered under her breath, "Men. And all they'll never have to suffer…"

"I do sympathize."

"Why doesn't that help?"

She left him to comfort the squalling Rosie as she hobbled outside to the bathroom, where she used the facilities, changed her menstrual pad and then forced herself to straighten her spine. Every overworked muscle protested. But she did it. And she stayed upright all the way back to the main room.

Logan built up last night's fire and got started on the breakfast as Lacey and Rosie practiced nursing. By the time she'd changed the baby—on the bureau/changing table that Zach had brought over while she was sleeping—Logan was cracking eggs into a pan.

"How many?" he asked.

"Four."

He laughed. "I see you've gotten over your aversion to eggs."

"And toast, please. And juice and some of that applesauce that's up in the cupboard. And maybe, after that, a big bowl of cereal…"

Tess and Edna arrived at a little after ten. By then, Rosie had been through three diaper changes and two more short nursing sessions. Between the feeding and the changing, Lacey faded in and out of a drowsy half-sleep. She felt sore and tired and utterly content, with her baby in her arms and Logan to take care of them both.

Tess and Edna told Lacey she was not to get up. She ignored them and pulled on her robe. "I need to move around a little." She tried not to groan as she pulled herself straight for the walk across the floor to the rocking chair.

The visitors each held Rosie, cooing over her shamelessly and declaring her the most beautiful child they'd ever seen.

Lacey couldn't help laughing—which hurt her poor tummy. "Why is it people always say that new babies are beautiful? They have rashy red skin and squashed faces and this one even has a point on the top of her head."

Edna was holding Rosie right then. She clucked her tongue and rocked back and forth. "There, there," she told the baby, "don't you listen to Mommy. She knows you're beautiful. She just doesn't want you to become vain about it. And don't you worry about this point on your head. It won't be there for long." She stroked Rosie's fuzzy head. "Of course, Jobeth and Starr can't wait to meet you…"

Tess added, smiling at Lacey, "We told them maybe tomorrow, after you've both had a little more time to recuperate."

When they were through fussing over the baby, they handed her back to Lacey and enlisted Logan's aid in making up a grocery list. "We're going into town this afternoon," Edna said. "We'll pick up whatever you need. Anything else we can do?"

Jenna, Lacey thought. She stopped her lazy rocking. Over eight hours since Rosie had come into the world and her Aunt Jenna didn't even know that the momentous event had occurred.

Lacey shot a swift, guilty glance at Logan—and then instantly wondered what was the matter with her. She was not going to put off sharing the wonderful news with her sister just because the mention of Jenna's name might cause Logan a little emotional discomfort.

She spoke firmly. "You can take me over to the main house for a few minutes. I need to make a phone call to Florida, to give Jenna and Mack the news."

Edna frowned in disapproval. "But don't you have one of those portable phones?"

Lacey put Rosie on her shoulder, pushed herself from the rocker and drew her sore body up tall. "I hate to use a cell phone. When it does work, it tends to cut in and out. And then there's an irritating delay on and off, too. It's no fun trying to talk on it, especially for something like this. Logan, if you'll take the baby, I'll just get into some clothes and then—"

Edna clucked her tongue and bustled over. "You sit back down, young lady. You're in no shape to go traipsing down the road right yet."

Logan and Tess stayed where they were, over by the counter. Neither of them spoke—Logan for reasons Lacey didn't really want to examine. And Tess...well, Lacey had told her about Logan's feelings for Jenna just yesterday. No doubt Tess didn't know what to say.

But Edna was blithely ignorant of the emotional minefield they were forging across here. "Why don't you let Logan or Tess make the call for you right now? Then you can call again yourself in a day or two, when you're feeling up to it."

Tess finally decided to speak up. "Uh, Edna, I think Lacey wants to be the one to give her sister the big news."

Lacey sent Zach's wife a grateful smile. "Yes, I do. I want to tell her myself. And if you'll just drive me over there and then drive me back...please. It won't take long. I'm sure I'm up to it."

She glanced Logan's way again. His face betrayed nothing—not the usual concern for her welfare, and certainly not whatever emotions all this talk about

Jenna called up in him. "Logan, do you think you could look after Rosie on your own for a little while?"

He did move then. He strode toward her. "I think I can handle it." His voice, like his expression, gave her nothing. But at least he wasn't trying to talk her out of it. He took Rosie from her, carefully laying a diaper and then the baby on his broad shoulder.

Lacey found herself staring at his fine, large hands, thinking how small—and how safe—their daughter looked cradled in them. Her love was an ache right then. It filled her with warmth—and it hurt, too.

"Great," Lacey said brightly. "I'll be dressed in a flash."

Tess let Lacey use the phone in Zach's office, off the dining room, where she could close the door and enjoy complete privacy.

Her sister answered on the second ring. Just the sound of that soft, clear voice brought tears to Lacey's eyes.

"Hello?"

"Jen. It's me."

"Lace. Hello."

Lacey closed her eyes, picturing her big sister's gorgeous wide-open smile. Nobody smiled quite like Jenna. Nobody in the world.

Lacey said, "So tell me. How are you feeling?"

Jenna laughed. "Great. Considering I'm as big as a house. How about you?"

Lacey breathed deep. "Well, let me put it this way. *I'm* not quite as big today as I was yesterday."

Jenna gasped. "The baby? You had the—"

"Yes. This morning at about two. A baby girl. Seven pounds, two ounces."

"Omigod. I can't believe it. How do you feel? Are you okay? You're calling from the hospital, then? And the baby. How is the baby?"

"We're both fine. I'm at the main ranch house now. Tess brought me over, to call you. We never made it to the hospital. I had the baby in the cabin."

"Oh, dear Lord. You didn't."

"I did. It all happened really fast. I went to sleep at around eleven last night and I woke up when my water broke, two hours later. And an hour after that, I was holding my baby in my arms. And she's perfect. Absolutely beautiful...even if she is the ugliest thing I've ever seen."

Jenna was laughing and sighing at the same time. "Oh, Lace. I...I don't have the words. Hold on. I have to tell Mack."

Lacey heard her sister call her husband, then the excited exchange of information. Then Mack came on the line. "Congratulations, sister-in-law."

She smiled. "Thanks, Mack."

"Take it easy, now. Get lots of rest."

"Yeah. With a newborn. Right."

"Well, get as much rest as you can, at least—and I have to go now. Jenna's trying to rip the phone out of my hands."

"Bye, Mack."

"Take care."

"Tell me you named her after Mother—" it was Jenna again "—that you didn't forget what we agreed."

"How could I forget? If I had a girl, she'd be Mar-

garet. If I didn't and *you* did, then my *niece* would be
Margaret. I did. So she's Margaret. Margaret Rose.
We're calling her Rosie."

"Rosie. I like it."

It didn't even occur to Lacey to dissemble. Not with
Jenna. She could tell Jenna anything. "Maybe you remember. Rose was Logan's mother's name."

"Of course I remember. And I think it's a good
choice."

Lacey gulped. "He's here, Jenna."

A pause. "You mean Logan?"

"Uh-huh."

"You finally told him."

"And he came right away."

"Naturally. Oh, Lace. I'm so glad you did it."

"You know what? So am I."

"Will you marry him? He *has* asked you, hasn't he?"

"Demanded is more like it. I told him no. About a
hundred times. I finally got him to back off on the subject, as a condition of letting him stick around."

"So what are you saying? You won't marry him?
You're firm on that?"

"Oh, Jen. I *was* firm. At first. But he's been…so in-
credibly supportive. Right with me through everything.
True and steady, you know how he is. The kind of man
you can lean on, count on, through the toughest times,
no matter what."

"Yes. Yes, I do know."

"A total ant."

"What?"

Lacey laughed. "Oh, nothing." And then she felt her

smile fade. She clutched the phone tighter. "I...I told him. That I love him."

"That's good."

"You think so?"

"Absolutely."

"He still loves you, Jenna."

"Did he say that?"

"No, but I know he does."

"You're assuming."

"Stop. You sound like Tess."

"You talked with Tess about it? What did she say?"

"She said I should say yes. That Logan and I should get married and I should...give love a place to grow."

Jenna sighed. "Give love a place to grow. I like that."

"So do I. Probably too much. Having a baby has turned me into a sentimental fool."

"You love him. He wants to marry you. He will be good to you, Lacey. I know that he will. And if he doesn't know that he loves you now, he'll figure it out, if you give it time."

"But he *doesn't* love me. He loves—"

"Lace."

"What?"

"I want you to listen to me. Listen to me closely."

Lacey shifted the phone to her other ear and grumbled, "What?"

"I know that man."

"I'm aware of that."

"Don't become defensive. Please."

Lacey shifted the phone back where she'd had it before. "All right. I'm sorry. It's a sensitive subject for me."

"I know. And maybe you don't want to hear this now. Is that it? You had a baby a few hours ago and the last thing you need right now is a lecture from your big sister."

"You know, that's true, I really don't want to hear it. I'll probably never want to hear it. But I probably *should* hear it, for my own good, right?"

"Does that mean you're listening?"

"Yes. Go on. I can take it."

Jenna let a moment of silence elapse. Then she started over. "I know Logan. And I tried, for so long, to love him the way that you do, because I thought that he and I were right for each other. He thought so, too. And when Logan Severance gets an idea in his head, well, you know what he's like."

Lacey made a noise of agreement. "Do I ever. Certain words come to mind—'relentless' among them."

"Exactly. He never gives up. And he's loyal until death. These are wonderful qualities. But they can also make it so a man can't see the nose in front of his face."

Lacey couldn't help interjecting, "The man is bull-headed."

Her sister thoroughly agreed. "That would be the word. You know how he was in high school. Every girl's dream. Handsome to die for, kind to everyone and her mother, and destined for professional success. Even after he and I started going steady, all the other girls were after him. Some of them were shameless. But I never felt jealous. I knew he had made up his mind to love me and he wouldn't even look twice at any of them. He didn't. In fact, there's only one other woman he ever seemed to pay more attention to than he did to me."

Lacey had been wrapping the phone cord slowly around her finger. She pulled it free. "Logan? Give more than the time of day to a woman who wasn't you? Never."

"Yes, he did."

"Who?"

"You."

Lacey let out a low cry of disbelief. "That's ridiculous."

"No. Think about it. He was always and forever asking about you. Sometimes it used to really get on my nerves." Jenna cleared her throat and imitated Logan's deep voice. "'How's Lacey? Don't tell me she's run away again? When is she going to take her schoolwork more seriously? Don't you think it's about time she stopped getting into trouble? She needs a college education. And I think we ought to talk to her about getting herself a real job...' And on and on and on. I'm telling you, it never stopped."

Lacey couldn't see how that added up to proof of Logan's romantic interest in her. "He was just playing big brother, that's all."

"He took the role a little too seriously, if you ask me. In fact, in retrospect, it seems to me that he took it *way* too seriously. Did it ever occur to you that maybe he's been crazy about you for years now and he's just too obstinate to admit that he chose the wrong sister? After all, he's Logan Severance. And Logan Severance is perfect. He doesn't make mistakes."

"Jen. I always got on his nerves. He wanted to reform me."

"He wanted to do a lot more than reform you—he just wouldn't admit it to himself."

"Wait a minute. I'm starting to see the light here. You're saying all this because you think I should say yes to him."

"I'm saying it because I think it's true."

"You know, I can't help recalling what I told you last September—that if I thought Logan loved me, then nothing could keep me away from him."

"Lace. I have not made all this up to get you to marry him. I honestly haven't. I've been thinking a lot about this and I truly believe there's something to it. *You're* the one Logan really wants."

"And *you* are my big sister, who loves me and thinks I'd be better off if I married the nice, handsome, stable M.D. who is the father of my baby—even if he *is* still in love with you."

Jenna let out a grunt of pure frustration. "I could easily become perturbed with you. He's not in love with me. He only thinks he is."

Lacey wasn't buying. "And what *is* love anyway, but something you think? Where else does it exist… except in a person's mind, in whatever it is we call the 'heart'?"

"No," Jenna said. "I'm sorry. I can't agree with you on that."

"What's not to agree with?"

"Most of all, love is what you *do*. It's a verb. An action word. If you really love, you behave in a loving way."

That hit home. Lacey stared out the window at the side yard, where a few of Tess's chickens pecked the ground. In the distance, off to the northwest, the snowy crests of the Big Horn Mountains reflected back the morning sun.

If love came down to action, she could find no fault with the way that Logan Severance "loved" her. As soon as she'd told him about the baby, he'd put his life and his work on hold to come to her. He'd looked after her from the moment of his arrival here. He'd delivered their baby, and he'd done a beautiful job of it. Now, he was back at the cabin, watching the baby, while she broke the news of the birth to her sister—who also just happened to be the woman who had left him for another man.

"Lace. You still there?"

"I'm here."

"Will you just think about what I said?"

"Yes. I will. I'll think about it."

"I do understand how *you* are, too, Lace. How important your independence is to you, how you've never been one to take the traditional way. Maybe the real issue here is that marriage just isn't for you."

"I never said marriage wasn't for me. I've always thought I *would* marry. Someday. When the right man came along."

"To me it seems pretty obvious that Logan *is* the right man."

"I'm getting that loud and clear."

Jenna took in a long breath and let it out slowly. "Listen. Remember how you told me once that there was something lukewarm between me and Logan?"

"Jenna—"

"Just bear with me for a minute more. Do you remember?"

"Yes. All right. I remember."

"And remember how you laughed when I admitted that Logan and I had never made love?"

"It surprised me, that's all."

"Because you couldn't imagine anyone passing up the chance to be in his arms. Am I right?"

"I didn't think that at the time. I swear."

"I know you didn't, not consciously. Then, he was *my* fiancé, after all. But now. Looking back on it. What do you think now?"

"All right," Lacey conceded reluctantly. "Maybe."

"Maybe what?"

"Jenna, you have made your point. And I really have to—"

"You have to go. I know. But please. Just think about what I've said."

"I will. I promise."

"Great. And kiss my niece for me."

"Will do."

"I can't wait to meet her."

"Soon," Lacey said, and felt a sudden tightness in her chest.

Would it really be soon? She and Jenna lived on opposite sides of the country now. Lacey had a new baby and Jenna was fast approaching her own delivery date. For a while, anyway, life itself would get in the way of their visiting each other.

And if Lacey did marry Logan...

Well, then, it would probably be awkward at best and

awful at worst, for her and Logan to get together with Jenna and Mack.

"Soon," Lacey said again, in an effort to convince herself that she meant it.

"Yes," Jenna replied softly. "We'll have to get together soon...."

Chapter 7

When Tess drove her back to the cabin, Lacey made her cousin's wife let her off in the dusty turnaround out front. "I can walk to the door myself. I'm not an invalid."

Tess shook her head. "You're a wonder, that's what you are. A few hours out of childbed and you're strolling around the yard."

Lacey climbed down from the pickup slowly. "It's only ten yards to the door—and I don't think 'stroll' is exactly the word for it."

"You won't be mad if I just wait here until you get inside?"

"I guess I'll allow that." She *was* feeling a little tired. And the cramping in her uterus had increased a bit. She wanted to lie down and sleep for about a week.

"Edna and I will be back around five, with the groceries. And tell Logan not to cook. We'll bring something over."

"I'll tell him. And thanks. For everything."

"Any time."

Lacey hobbled toward the door. It opened before she got there and Logan came out.

Tess waved and drove off.

"You look beat," Logan said, as he took her arm.

"I'm a little tired, I admit." She leaned on him heavily, grateful for his solid strength, as he led her inside.

Miracle of miracles, Rosie was asleep. She lay on her side in her bassinet, making little sucking motions with her tiny pink mouth.

"I'm just going to go out to the bathroom for a minute," Lacey whispered. "And then I'll lie down."

Dark eyes narrowed. "Is something wrong?"

"I think I'm bleeding a little more than before."

She felt certain that he would reprimand her then, that he'd say she'd been foolish to insist on a visit to the main house just to call Jenna.

But he surprised her. He put his hand on her shoulder, a touch clearly meant to comfort. It had the intended effect. She did feel reassured. She put her hand over his and gave it a squeeze.

"Sometimes the bleeding can be pretty heavy," he said, "especially in the first few days. It's probably nothing to worry about. You can change your pad and put your nightgown back on and come lie down. You'll feel better after you've rested a while."

Logan was right. She did feel better after she'd rested. He brought her the baby about an hour later and he helped her to sit up against the pillows to nurse.

He didn't ask her what she and her sister had said to each other. He didn't mention the call to Jenna at all. Which was all right with her. Lacey didn't really want to discuss the call with him, anyway.

She was quiet as the day wore on.

She had a lot to think about. With Rosie in her arms and Logan by her side, she found herself beginning to see her life in a whole new light.

Perhaps, to an extent, she *had* been irresponsible—living day-to-day, taking things as they came. But now so much had changed.

Through the rest of the morning and into the afternoon, her sister's words stayed with her. She wondered, could they be true? Was she, Lacey, the one Logan *really* loved?

In any case, she certainly did admire Jenna's definition of the word—of it being what people *did* that mattered, not what they said, or even whatever secrets they kept hidden in their hearts.

And Jenna and Tess both thought she should say yes to Logan. Could two such wise and wonderful women be wrong?

That evening, Tess and Edna returned, but only long enough to carry in the groceries and put the dinner on the table. Once they were gone, Logan called to Lacey through the curtain, asking if she'd like him to serve her meal in bed.

"No way," she called back. "I'll eat at the table. This bed rest is getting to me."

"You're sure?"

"Positive. I'll be right out." She wrapped herself in her robe and joined him in the main room.

He was standing at the counter. "Look what I found." He held up two saucers. A plain votive candle was perched on each one. He carried the saucers to the table, set them in the center and produced a wooden match, which he struck with a flourish on the underside of the tabletop.

The sulfur tip hissed as the flame caught. "Dinner by candlelight," he announced as he lit one wick and then the other. He shook out the match. "There."

It was a whimsical gesture, something she never would have expected of him. He *was* a generous man and he knew what women liked. He used to send flowers to Jenna all the time. And during those five glorious days last September, he had taken Lacey out to dinner twice, each time to a fine restaurant, where there were always candles on the snowy linen tablecloth—not to mention champagne chilling in a silver bucket nearby.

But he'd never done a tender thing like this for her— to create a little impromptu romance at a rough pine table with a couple of squat white votives scrounged from a drawer.

It touched her. It touched her deeply.

He pulled out her chair for her and then, when they were seated with the candles glowing between them, he raised his big glass of milk to her in a toast.

"To the mother of my daughter," he said. "A woman with an independent mind and...unquenchable determination."

She laughed. "Independence and determination. I like it."

"I knew that you would."

She raised her glass and they drank at the same time.

Then she thought of a toast of her own. "To the father of my little girl. A man of…unflagging loyalty and truly staggering persistence."

"Loyalty and persistence." He saluted her by dipping his head. "Admirable qualities. Thank you."

She nodded. "You're welcome." They drank again.

When they set down their glasses, Lacey said softly, "Why do I know what's coming?"

He smiled rather ruefully. "You have to admit, I've shown admirable restraint for—what—at least forty-eight hours now?"

"Yes, Logan. You have."

"But my goal hasn't changed. And it does seem to me that maybe you've been rethinking my offer."

"You could be right."

"*Could* be?"

"You'll have to ask to find out."

He studied her face for a moment, then asked gravely, "Would I increase my chances for success if I went down on my knees?"

"Hmm…" She pretended to consider the question, but she didn't pretend for long. "I love to see a man down on his knees."

His expression remained solemn, though humor gleamed in his eyes. "I don't believe I'll comment on that remark."

"A wise decision. One you will not regret."

He set down his napkin and pushed back his chair.

In two steps, he was standing beside her. He wore jeans and a dark knit shirt with a banded collar. She thought he had never looked more handsome. But then, every time she looked at him, she found herself thinking that he had never looked more handsome.

He dropped to one knee. "May I have your hand, please?"

She gave it. He bent his dark head. She felt the warm, quick brush of his lips against her knuckles.

Then he was staring up at her again, his eyes so dark, shining with—maybe not love—but something almost as good.

"Ms. Bravo."

She dipped her head and matched his teasingly formal tone, "Dr. Severance."

"Ms. Bravo, much has transpired between us in recent hours. So much, in fact, that my humble hopes have been raised once again."

She arched a brow at him. "Humble? Your hopes are *humble?*"

He gave her a quick, playful scowl—then resumed looking ardent once more. "I would like your hand in marriage, Ms. Bravo."

"No. Really?"

"Yes. Really."

She sucked in a big breath and let it out in a rush. "This is *such* a surprise."

He kissed her hand again. A lovely shiver traveled up her arm. "I can provide for you."

"Ah." She sighed some more, a couple of big, gusty ones. "You're a man with… prospects?"

"Better than that."

"Better?" She fluttered her eyelashes madly. "Do elaborate."

He made a big show of clearing his throat. "Well. All right. If you insist."

"I do. Most definitely. Don't be shy. Enumerate your assets."

"First let me say that my assets are…at your disposal."

"Oh, this is sounding better by the minute. Don't stop now. Go on, go on."

"Well, I own a house. And I've made wise investments."

"What about all that lovely money your father left you?"

"Yes. There's that, too."

"Hmm. This is good. Continue."

"I don't think I'd be exaggerating if I told you that I hold a position of respect in my community."

"Your community." She frowned. "That would be… Meadow Valley, California?"

"Yes. Meadow Valley. In California."

She allowed herself a slow, very significant grin. "I have something of a reputation myself, in Meadow Valley."

His fine mouth twitched, though he kept a straight face. "Yes, I've heard. But I'm willing to overlook that."

"Such a generous fellow you are, Dr. Severance."

"So I've been told…and where was I?"

"You hold a position of respect…"

"Ah, yes. In Meadow Valley. Also gainful employment."

"Always a plus."

"And then there's the fact that you've just had my baby. I don't think we should forget that."

She placed her hand, very delicately, over her stomach. "I promise you. I haven't forgotten."

"And then there are…those tender feelings I bear you."

Now *that* did sound good. "Tender feelings? I find you are persuading me, Dr. Severance. You are quite wonderfully convincing."

He rose then, in one quick, easy movement. He looked down into her eyes and she watched his expression change, from one of playful devotion to something darker and hungrier.

He said her name. "Lace…"

A shudder ran through her.

"…come up here."

He tugged on her hand, pulling her out of her chair and into his strong arms. She groaned—because it hurt to stand up straight. And also because it felt so absolutely grand to be in his arms again at last.

"Marry me, damn it."

"Oh, Logan…"

He lowered his mouth. It touched hers. He said it again, breathing the words into her mouth. "Marry me."

And then he kissed her.

There was no one—no one—who kissed the way Logan kissed.

She had missed his kisses terribly. Sometimes, in the night, alone, during the months apart from him, she would wake and touch her mouth and remember….

She had thought, for all those long, long months, that she would never feel his kisses again.

But here she was. Feeling them. Taking them into herself, kissing him back.

Her lips felt deliciously bruised when he finally pulled away. She reached up, put her fingers against them.

He commanded for a third time, in a low, very controlled tone, "Marry me."

She opened her mouth to answer.

And from her bassinet in the corner, Rosie started crying.

Lacey moved instinctively toward the sound.

Logan gripped her arms, holding her with him. "Wait," he whispered, "maybe she'll just go back to sleep."

"No. I know that sound. She's hungry."

Heat still burned in his eyes, but one corner of his mouth kicked up in a wry half-smile. "You know that sound? Already?"

"'Fraid so."

"Just wait a minute, though. Just in case?"

"All right."

They waited, staring at each other like a pair of smitten lovers which, Lacey admitted to herself right then, was what they were.

Rosie went on wailing.

Finally, Logan shrugged. "All right." He let her go and she turned for the bassinet.

She waited until she was seated in the rocker with the baby at her breast before she looked up at Logan standing above her and softly whispered, "Yes."

Chapter 8

The next day, when Tess brought Jobeth and Starr over to see the baby, Lacey and Logan delivered their news.

"Oh, this is wonderful." Tess grabbed Lacey in a hug. "When will the ceremony be?"

"Right away," said Logan. "We'll get the blood tests tomorrow. And as soon as I can coax the results out of whoever runs the local lab, we'll pay a visit to the county courthouse—Wednesday or Thursday, that would be my guess."

But the women had other ideas. Surely Logan could wait a few days at least, until Lacey was recovered enough to enjoy her own wedding? And there really should be some sort of party, something small and simple, understandably, on such short notice. Something with only the family, but a real ceremony none-theless....

* * *

On Monday morning, Logan drove into Buffalo and came back with a safety seat for Rosie. It took him half an hour to do it, but he finally got the thing properly strapped into the back of Lacey's SUV. Then he loaded mother and daughter into the vehicle and they went to the clinic in Medicine Creek, where Lacey and Logan had their blood tests and Dr. Pruitt produced Rosie's birth certificate, all ready for her parents to sign.

They got back to the cabin two hours after they'd left it. Lacey and the baby took a nap and Logan went to the main house, where he called his office and promised Dan Connery, one of his two overworked partners, that he'd be back in Meadow Valley the following week.

"The problem—whatever it is—is solved, then?" Dan asked, sounding more than a little put out about the whole thing.

Logan took full blame for his partner's frustration. He'd been far from forthcoming about why he'd suddenly found it imperative to fly off to Wyoming for an indefinite stay. He needed to sit down with Dan and Helen Sanderson, the third partner in the practice, and explain what had happened.

He wasn't looking forward to the task. He found the whole situation more than a little embarrassing.

After all, he *was* a doctor. A respected member of his community. A man others rightfully expected to uphold certain standards.

The way Logan saw it, a doctor should never have the bad judgment to become a father *before* he'd managed to marry the mother of his child. Certain…restraint was expected of a physician. And if a physician couldn't exercise restraint, well, he ought at least to know better than to slip up when it came to the use of contraception.

But Logan *had* slipped up. And Dan and Helen had a right to an explanation. There would no doubt be gossip anyway, when Logan returned to town with a new wife *and* a baby.

And then there was the fact that his bride just happened to be his ex-fiancée's younger sister—a younger sister who had once been well-known in Meadow Valley for her exploits as a troubled teen.

Yes, there would be talk. And his partners not only deserved to hear the truth from him, they had a right to hear it from him *first*.

He would see that they did. As soon as he returned.

"I'm…working things out, Dan," Logan said. "I'll explain everything, in detail, as soon as I get back."

"All right. Next Monday, then?"

Monday wouldn't work, and Logan knew it. He and Lacey were getting married on Saturday. There would be a party, which would mean some degree of stress for her. Better to give her Sunday to rest.

And then she had that new SUV of hers. He doubted she'd be willing to leave it in Wyoming. And really, with Rosie so young, it was probably wiser not to try flying anyway. So they'd be driving. That would take two days at least—no, again, he had to consider Rosie. Traveling with a baby could be very slow going. Better give it three.

"Let's say Thursday, to be on the safe side. I'll be driving back and should get in by Wednesday evening."

Dan agreed that Thursday would be all right, though

he sounded far from thrilled about it. "Please don't make it any longer than that, Logan."

Sending a quick prayer heavenward that nothing would occur to make him into a liar, Logan promised he'd be there by a week from Thursday.

The next morning, Lacey drove to the main house—by herself this time—to call Jenna and tell her about the wedding.

Jenna was thoroughly pleased at the news. "I'm so glad, Lace. I really do think it's the best thing."

"Well, I hope so. Because I'm doing it."

"And what then? That big, beautiful house of Logan's in Meadow Valley?"

Lacey gulped. "Yep. Can you believe it? Wasn't I the one who swore I'd never move back to my hometown?"

"Never say never," Jenna teased.

"Ain't that the truth."

"And Meadow Valley is a beautiful place to live."

"Well, *you* always liked it there."

"It's kind of ironic." Jenna's voice held a wistful note. "All I ever wanted was to spend my life there. And all you ever wanted was to get out. And look at us now."

"No, Jen," Lacey said, "you wanted Mack more than you wanted to live in Meadow Valley. And me? Well, look who *I* ended up wanting."

Jenna laughed. "Mr. Meadow Valley himself. What did I tell you?"

Lacey was nodding. "Pure irony."

"You'll be all right," Jenna said. "You'll have the man you love and your baby. And there are four bedrooms in that house of Logan's—five if you include the upstairs family room. I'm sure one of them is going to make a great studio. You'll be totally absorbed in some new painting project again before you know it."

"Right," Lacey said. At that point, the idea of starting a new painting seemed far off in the distant future somewhere.

Which was nothing to worry about. After all, it had only been a few days since she'd had her baby. Right now, all she could think of was her child and her new life with Logan.

"Lace," Jenna said, "be happy. Take care of yourself."

Lacey promised that she would.

"Call me if you need me. Any time. For anything."

"I will. I promise."

After she hung up, Lacey realized that neither of them had brought up the idea of Jenna and Mack flying west for the wedding, though Mack was a multimillionaire who set his own schedule and Jenna's job right then consisted of renovating the old mansion they owned in Key West. They could have easily managed the trip.

But it wouldn't have been practical, Lacey told herself. It was such short notice, after all. And Jenna *was* seven months pregnant. Maybe she didn't feel up to any serious traveling at this point.

It wouldn't have been practical....

Lacey sat back in her cousin's leather desk chair and shook her head at the phoniness of her own excuses.

Practicality wasn't the issue.

The issue was that she didn't want the woman Logan had loved for fifteen years at her wedding—even if that woman did happen to be her own wonderful big sister.

Lacey had a feeling the idea didn't hold much appeal for Jenna, either. Or maybe Jenna was just being considerate and would have come in a minute if Lacey had only asked her.

Whatever.

Someday, they would all have to deal with this uncomfortable situation.

Someday.

But not right now.

Right now, there was too much to deal with already. A new baby. A new husband. A new life in her old hometown.

She got up from the chair, pushed it under the big desk and went out to thank Tess for the use of the phone.

All the local Bravos showed up for the wedding. Cash and Abby and their little boy, Tyler. And another cousin, Nate, who brought his wife Meggie and their toddler, Jason James. Meggie had a cousin of her own named Sonny. Sonny had a wife and two kids. They all came, too.

The honorable Reverend Applegate, who, as it turned out, had presided at the weddings of Cash and Abby *and* Tess and Zach, performed the ceremony. He kept it simple and brief.

Lacey gaped in disbelief when Logan slipped a diamond ring on her finger. Now, where had he found the time to go out and buy that? He must have read her thoughts in her expression, because he leaned close and whispered, "I bought it in Meadow Valley, the day before I flew out here to get you."

She stared down at the lovely bright stone glittering on her finger, then whispered back, "Pretty sure of yourself, weren't you?"

He answered with a question of his own. "Do you like it?"

And she had to confess, "I do. Oh, Logan. Thank you. I like it very much."

The Reverend Applegate coughed to get their attention. "And now," the reverend intoned, "You may kiss the bride."

Logan kissed her. Pure heaven, Logan's kiss. She threw her arms around him and kissed him back.

The Reverend had to cough again to remind them that they'd been kissing long enough. As they drew apart, Lacey heard chuckling from more than one of the guests. And sniffling, too—Edna or Tess, probably.

After the ceremony, they all sat down to dinner at the long table in the dining room. Tess and Edna had put out the best china and silver. There were candles, twelve in all, thin white tapers in antique silver candlesticks. In their warm light, the china gleamed and the fine, old family linen gave off an ivory glow.

The cousins and their wives took turns toasting the happy couple.

"To Lacey and Logan…"

"To the bride and groom…"

"To happiness…"

"Eternal love…"

Logan laid his hand over Lacey's. She twined her fingers with his.

It will all work out, she told herself. I love him and he…well, he cares for me. And he wants to take care of me. And there's Rosie. She needs us both. I'll take Tess's advice, she promised herself, as Zach stood to propose another toast.

I'll do everything I can to give love a place to grow....

Chapter 9

They left for California early Monday morning, Logan following behind Lacey in his rental car to Buffalo, where he'd made arrangements to drop the car off.

In Buffalo, Logan took the wheel of the SUV. They made surprisingly good time the first day, considering that they had a newborn as a passenger. They stayed in Salt Lake City that night, in a nice hotel that provided excellent room service. They ate by candlelight, in the sitting room of their suite.

Lacey said, "This is getting to be a habit with us, romantic dinners with candles on the table...." She had her shoes off by then and she reached out her toe and hooked it under the cuff of Logan's trouser leg.

He gave her a smoldering look from under those sinfully thick, dark lashes of his. "If you keep that up, you won't get a chance to finish your dinner."

She laughed, a thoroughly naughty laugh, a laugh that made his dark eyes smolder all the more.

Of course, it was too soon after Rosie's birth to make love in the fullest sense. But Lacey had always been an imaginative woman. She liked giving pleasure as much as she enjoyed receiving it.

On their wedding night, by the time they finally got into bed together in the cabin, she'd been too tired to think of anything but curling up close to Logan and trying to catch a few winks before Rosie woke and demanded feeding again. But in the morning she'd felt a little friskier. She'd been able to remind her new husband of how much he appreciated what she could do with her lips and her hands.

She'd reminded him more than once since then.

He said she was insatiable.

She patiently explained to him that, no, *he* was insatiable. She was merely helpful.

"Eat your dinner," he commanded gruffly.

She shrugged and picked up her fork.

Later, after Rosie had been fed and diapered for what seemed like the hundredth time that day, Logan took Lacey's hand and led her to the king-size bed. She had planned, once again, to show him just how helpful she could be.

But her body, evidently, wasn't quite so willing as her mind. She closed her eyes when her head hit the pillow. And that was it. She didn't open them again until Rosie started crying for her next feeding.

Tuesday, they ended up in Winnemucca, Nevada. They shared a pizza in the room and fell asleep watching television—with the sound down very low, of course, in order not to disturb their slumbering daughter.

Wednesday, they were on the road good and early. In Reno, at a little after eleven o'clock, they made a brief stop at the airport to pick up Logan's Cadillac. And by early Wednesday afternoon, Lacey was pulling her SUV into the tree-shaded driveway of Logan's two-story house in Meadow Valley, just a block and a half from the old Queen Anne Victorian where she had grown up. Logan nosed his Cadillac in beside her.

He had their luggage and all the baby's things out of the back of the SUV and stacked in the skylighted two-story front foyer in no time at all. "I thought we'd put Rosie in the east bedroom, the one that overlooks the back deck. It's the closest one to the master suite, so that'll minimize the running back and forth."

"Sounds fine," Lacey said. "The closer the better."

Rosie was right there in the foyer with them, lying on her back in the bassinet that Tess had given her, making little cooing sounds and staring up toward the skylight.

"She's happy," Lacey said. "Let's get moving before she decides she's hungry again." She picked up a big suitcase.

Logan took it from her. "No heavy lifting for you."

She made a face at him. "I'm fine."

"Take that stack of baby blankets and come on. You can start putting things in drawers while I carry it all up there."

"We'll have to fix this room up for a baby," Logan said half an hour later, as Lacey was changing their daughter on the queen-size bed in the room Logan had chosen for her. "We need a crib, and a changing table—"

Lacey nodded. "And a dresser or two, some cute kid's-room curtains, new paint—the works." She pressed the tab on the diaper and straightened Rosie's little pink T-shirt. "There. All clean."

Logan said, "Listen…"

She put the baby on her shoulder and smiled at him. "What?"

"I want to check in at my office for a while. Will you be all right?"

"Sure."

"The refrigerator should be fully stocked." He had called his housekeeper, Mrs. Hopper, before they left Wyoming, to ask her to have everything ready for them.

"I'll be fine," Lacey said.

"I need to…have a talk with my partners. I thought maybe I'd take them to dinner, if I can catch them and they can make the time."

Dinner? That was hours away. "You'll be gone until sometime in the evening, then? Is that what you're saying?" She really did try not to sound as bewildered as his sudden decision to take off for so long made her feel.

"Lace. I've left them high and dry for two weeks— after giving them virtually no notice that I was leaving and no reason why. I only said I had some personal problems that couldn't wait. I owe them an explanation and I want to get it taken care of as soon as possible."

Lacey forced an understanding smile. "Hey. It's okay, really." And it was. If only she didn't feel so disoriented suddenly. As if she'd woken up and out of no-where found herself in some other woman's skin.

Lord. Married to Logan. The mother of his baby. Standing here in his beautiful house on Orchard Street with its spacious rooms and high ceilings, its sky-lights and arched windows, its walk-in closets in every room—the house where he and Jenna were supposed to have lived.

Logan was watching her, a frown marring his brow. "I'm sorry," he said. "If you're really uncomfortable with my leaving right now, it can wait until tomorrow."

Lacey shook herself. What was the matter with her? He was a doctor. If she couldn't get used to his being gone for long stretches of time, she'd be in big trouble.

And this *was* her hometown, for heaven's sake. If she got too lonely, she could call an old friend—one of the twins, her high school buddies, Mira or Maud.

But then again, maybe not. Not right away, anyway.

The twins *had* mellowed a lot in recent years. They no longer automatically despised anyone who embraced what they considered to be "establishment" values. But they still considered Logan something of a stuffed shirt. And Logan didn't think too highly of them, either.

She didn't know if she was ready right yet to listen to what they'd have to say to her when they learned that not only had she given birth to Mr. Straight-Arrow's baby, she'd gone and married him as well.

"Give me Rosie," Logan said. "I'll rock her for a while and you can go on in and lie down."

She granted him her best rebellious scowl. "Get out of here. Rosie and I can manage just fine."

Relief brought a smile to that sexy mouth of his. "You're sure?"

"Positive."

He leaned toward her and brushed a kiss at her temple. A moment later, he was gone.

Logan found Dan on duty at the office.

"Great. You're here." The other doctor clapped Logan heartily on the back. "Safe and sound. And a day early, too. Listen, I've got five of your patients scheduled for this afternoon, but since you're here now..." He let the suggestion finish itself.

"No problem. I'll take them."

"Good. And we'll need some consulting time, tomorrow morning, if possible. Get it out of the way. You've got a few surgeries to schedule and a mountain of charts we need to go over."

"Tomorrow morning's fine. Where's Helen?"

"She's already taken off for rounds at Miner's." All three had privileges at the local hospital, Miner's General.

"But she's coming back here later?"

"I think she said she'd drop back by around four-thirty, see if she could pick up the slack for me if I get too far behind. That shouldn't be a problem now, though, with you here."

"Right. No problem now—but I do need to ask a favor of both of you."

Dan rolled his eyes, but in a good-natured way. "Do not tell me you're taking off for another two weeks."

"I'm not. I just want to explain the details of my trip

to Wyoming. Can you clear off your calendar enough to let me buy you dinner tonight?"

"Tonight..." Dan said, considering. "I don't know. I'll have to check with Fiona." Fiona was Dan's wife of twenty-five years, a slender, gracious woman who chaired a number of volunteer organizations and loved to entertain. "Wednesdays are supposed to be our night out, just the two of us."

"Tell her it's all my fault and ask her to please forgive me. In fact, you're on call tomorrow night, right?"

"Right."

"You and Fiona can have it. I'll take the emergencies. We have to talk, Dan. As soon as Helen gets here, I'll ask her to join us, too."

"Is this...bad news?" Dan looked stricken.

Logan couldn't blame the other man for his reaction. Logan had joined the partnership just a few years ago, when the previous third partner had retired. As the junior member of the team, his partners rightfully expected him to take up the slack for them, to make their jobs easier. Since he'd learned that Lacey was pregnant, he hadn't been doing what they expected of him. It was only logical that Dan would now anticipate more of the same.

Logan hastened to reassure him. "No. It's not bad news, I promise you. It's just something you both need to be brought up to speed on, that's all."

Dan's expression relaxed. "Well. Good enough, then. I'll tell Fiona I'm all hers *tomorrow* night—and maybe tonight we could try Frau Angelica's? They say the rack of lamb there is out of this world."

"I'll get Cathy to call and make us a reservation."

Cathy was their extremely efficient receptionist. "Seven-thirty?"

"Better make it eight. I've got rounds of my own after I get through here."

"And I haven't been in to take a look at my desk yet, but I can guess that the in-box is stacked sky high."

"You imagine right." Dan affected a sigh.

"It's settled then. I'll have Cathy make the reservation for eight."

Reality check, Lacey kept thinking—or rather, *un*reality check. The afternoon had somehow turned into one long *un*reality check.

Her baby was demanding. But not *that* demanding. Rosie slept a lot. And while Rosie was sleeping, Lacey had plenty of time for wandering around Logan's house, meandering from one big, bright, beautifully appointed room to the next, wondering vaguely if this could really be her life.

Or if somehow, she had turned into Jenna.

Not the *real* Jenna, the strong, self-directed woman who had finally accepted her abiding love for Mack McGarrity and discovered that what she wanted most was a life at his side.

No, not that Jenna. But the other Jenna, the sweet, unassuming hometown girl who'd always known exactly how things would go for her: high school and then college in Los Angeles—just to get a taste of the big world out there. And then back to Meadow Valley to open a cute little shop, marry her high-school sweetheart and have a half-dozen kids.

Lacey could see Jenna's touch everywhere in the

house. All the curtains and area rugs, the towels in the bathrooms, even some of the furniture could have been bought at Linen and Lace, the shop Jenna had owned over on Commercial Street. A lot of the things no doubt *had* been bought there.

Logan had made an offer on the house three years ago. Lacey remembered Jenna mentioning the purchase. And over the months that followed, Jenna had helped him decorate it. They'd been dating again then, Jenna and Logan. And there had been a kind of unspoken understanding between them. That, eventually, he would ask. And she would say yes.

And then he *had* asked.

What neither of them had counted on was Mack McGarrity striding back into the picture, adding that key extra element that turned everything upside down.

Now, Jenna lived in Florida with Mack.

And Lacey lived with Logan in the house Jenna had decorated with the idea that someday it would be *her* house, too.

Strange. Bizarre. *Unreal.*

During the endless afternoon alone, while her daughter slept, Lacey went into each of the two unused bedrooms in turn. She stretched out on the beds and gazed at the ceilings. She looked in the closets and then stood at the windows, trying to picture herself creating a workspace there.

But in the end, she found herself staring at the curtains, or at an obviously expensive, hand-knotted rug on the hardwood floor.

She would stare and she would think: Jenna's choices.

Lacey never did decide which room to take. Probably the one in the southwest corner—it had windows on two sides and that meant more light.

But whichever room she chose, she would take down the pretty window treatments and banish the bed with its matching linens, its attractively contrasting tumble of throw pillows. The gorgeous area rugs would have to go. She would paint the walls eggshell white, install rice-paper blinds and leave the floors naked and shining, so that she could walk barefoot and feel the warm give of the wood beneath her soles.

After lingering for hours in each of the two unused bedrooms, she went down to the main floor. She wandered the dining room, the living room, the family room, thinking how lovely it all was, thinking...

*Un*reality check.

She stayed in the kitchen a long time, opening and closing the doors of the huge stainless-steel refrigerator, turning the big knobs on the chef-style range, gazing at the LaCuisine forged cutlery, mounted so cleverly on the wall over the green marble counter by means of a magnetized knife block.

Eventually, she opened the flatware drawer and stared at the forks.

And it happened.

One of those turn-around moments. The kind that occurs when you think you're driving south in some place you've never been before. You pass a landmark, something startlingly familiar.

And all of a sudden, you find you know right where you are. You've driven this route and you know it well.

And, wonder of wonders, you're going north—which is the direction you actually wanted to go.

Yes. A turn-around moment. Lacey looked at the forks in Logan's flatware drawer and all at once, she wasn't thinking of Jenna, or wondering if somehow she had taken over Jenna's life.

All at once, she was thinking strictly of herself. Standing naked in this very kitchen, tearing into a four-layer devil's food cake and feeding it to Logan, who happened to be just as naked as she.

By then, she was smiling.

And when she thought, *un*reality check, it was more with humor than with hurt.

At Frau Angelica's, after their entrées had been served, Logan embarked on the task of telling his partners everything he thought they needed to know.

He started out by saying that a few weeks ago, he'd learned that he was going to be a father. He'd gone to Wyoming with the intention of marrying the mother of his child.

"The baby, a little girl, was born Friday, the second," he explained. "And Lacey and I were married just this past Saturday."

He paused, to give the other two doctors a chance to say something.

Dan spoke up first, announcing way too cheerfully, "Well, this is certainly exciting news!"

Helen, who was in her mid-fifties but looked at least a decade younger, took a judicious sip of merlot. "Yes, Logan. Congratulations."

"Thank you."

Dan asked, "A daughter, you said?"

"Yes. Margaret Rose. We call her Rosie."

Helen said, "That's lovely. And your wife? Lacey...?"

"Bravo. Her last name was Bravo." He gave out that information fully expecting it to ring some bells.

It did. "Bravo?" Dan's right eyebrow shot toward his receding hairline. "I wonder. Is Lacey any relation to—?"

Logan let him have it. "As a matter of fact, Lacey is Jenna's younger sister."

Dan's jaw dropped. "Oh," he said. "Well, isn't that..." He didn't seem to know how to finish, so he coughed into his hand instead.

Both Dan and Helen had met Jenna on a number of occasions. They had each said they liked her immensely. Dan's wife had seemed very fond of her, too. As a matter of fact, Fiona had thrown a big engagement bash for Jenna and Logan. It had been a great party—and then three weeks later, Jenna had run off with Mack McGarrity.

Dan lurched to life and tried again. "This is just... such a surprise," he said.

A painful silence followed, during which Helen took on the task of buttering a kaiser roll and Dan evinced great interest in his rack of lamb.

Logan could almost hear their thoughts.

Hmm. Jenna left him. And that's when the sister came on the scene. An affair on the rebound. And the woman became pregnant. Now he's married her. I suppose he's made the best of a bad situation. But how long can it be expected to last?

Helen set her butter knife on the corner of her bread

plate. "I'm sure you're going to be very happy." She bit into her kaiser roll.

Logan did not flinch and he did not allow his eyes to shift away. "Yes. Lacey and I *are* very happy. And of course, we have the most beautiful baby in the world."

Helen finished chewing and swallowed. "I can't wait to meet both your wife and your daughter."

"And you will, I'm sure. Very soon."

Dan had recovered his equilibrium enough by then to exclaim, "I'm just stunned." He reached for the bottle in the center of the table and began topping off their glasses. "This calls for a toast." He set the bottle aside and raised his glass high. "Ahem. Here's to you, Logan. And to your bride. And your new daughter."

Logan thought of the long series of toasts at the Bravo table during his wedding dinner. He had liked those toasts better than Dan's. They'd seemed a lot more sincere.

Still, he had to admit that his partners were taking this pretty well.

And then again, why shouldn't they? The situation *was* something of an embarrassment, but nothing that couldn't be easily handled with the judicious application of proper damage control.

Helen raised her own glass and chimed in, "Yes, Logan. To your new family." She knocked back a big gulp of merlot.

Dan braced an elbow on the table and rubbed his chin. "I have an idea. Why doesn't Fiona give you and your bride a little party?"

Helen sat up straighter. "That's an excellent suggestion." She swung her sharp gaze Logan's way, then looked at Dan again. "But not a *small* party. A big one. A big party in honor of Logan's new family. Get Gabriella Rousseau to cater it. She's the best."

The corners of Dan's mouth drew down. His wife and her hostessing skills were a big asset to him, and he was always protective of her territory. "That's Fiona's department. She'll choose the caterer."

Helen dipped her perfectly groomed blond head. "Of course. It was just a thought."

"And I'll pass it right on to her."

"Great."

Dan was smiling, way too pleasantly. "You're quiet, Logan. Is a party a problem for you?"

A party, with most of the local medical community invited, no doubt, was probably not Lacey's idea of a great time. But he could talk her into it.

He'd have to warn her to be on her best behavior. She did have that wild side—the side his partners would most likely be hearing about once the gossip mill kicked in.

But for this, she'd tread the straight and narrow. For his sake. Because she did love him.

He had seen it in her eyes.

And heard it from her lips on the day that their daughter was born.

"Logan?" Dan was waiting for an answer.

"I think a party is an excellent idea, Dan. Thank you."

"No problem. Now, tell us some more about your new wife."

Logan set down his wineglass, thinking, she's reckless and a little wild and absolutely captivating. He said,

"Well, she's…a very adventurous woman. She's not afraid to take chances. She goes after what she wants."

"And what *does* she want?" Helen asked. The question was a particularly irritating mix of sly interest and condescension.

"She's lived in Los Angeles the last few years, pursuing a very promising career as an artist."

"An artist. How fascinating…"

Logan wished he were anywhere else right then but here at this restaurant discussing his private life with his professional colleagues.

He wished he were home. With Lacey.

Lacey.

All at once, he found himself holding back a fool's deep sigh as a swift series of images flashed on the screen of his mind.

Her incredible face, mottled and slick with sweat, grinning at him between the V of her spread legs on the night that their daughter was born.

What had she said right then?

It came to him: *"I feel so utterly demure…"*

And then later, not long after the birth, laying her palm against his cheek, confessing that she loved him.

And the night she finally said yes, giving him that grin of hers again across the rough pine table in that tiny, dark cabin, declaring, *"I have something of a reputation myself, in Meadow Valley…."*

Right then, he could almost wish himself back there with her, in that cramped little cabin, just the two of them and Rosie.

"Logan?" Helen was frowning at him. "Are you with us here?"

"Of course."

"We have to make some decisions. When should Fiona have that party?"

Logan pushed his tender thoughts aside and ordered his mind to focus on the all-important subject of damage control. "Let's give Lacey until her six-week check-up, how about that? Say, any time from mid-August on."

Dan asked, "Then Fiona *can* start making plans?"

"Absolutely."

Helen brought out her Palm Pilot and began punching buttons.

Logan glanced surreptitiously at his watch. Nine-fifteen.

What was she doing now? Nursing Rosie? He loved to watch that, her breast so white and full, traced with sweet blue veins, pressed against his daughter's plump cheek.

Or maybe she was lying in his bed, waiting for him? She might even be sleeping.

Since the baby, she seemed to have given up her passion for staying up until all hours. She'd learned to steal a nap whenever the opportunity presented itself.

Helen glanced up from the electronic device in her hand. "How does Saturday, the fourteenth, sound? Is that still too early?"

Dan was consulting his Day Runner. "For me, the fourteenth would probably be a go. Of course, I'll have to firm it up with Fiona."

Logan shrugged. "The fourteenth sounds fine to me."

Lacey had saved the master bedroom for last. She'd been in there to unload her suitcases, before Logan left. But after that, she hadn't crossed that particular threshold again. She'd waited until nine-thirty at night to return to it, first lingering over her solitary dinner, then hanging out in the family room for a while, watching a movie on HBO.

When she finally did enter the master suite, she went straight to the bath.

She showered in the enormous shower stall, glancing more than once at her soft, just-had-a-baby stomach and frowning, thinking that she'd have to put herself on some sort of exercise plan. Once she'd showered, she treated herself to a long, luxurious soak in the big spa tub.

After a while, resting her head back and closing her eyes, she let herself remember a few choice details of the five glorious days that had ended up creating Rosie and thus bringing her back here.

*Un*reality check.

Yes.

But what a beautiful time that had been.

Lacey heard Rosie crying just as she was drying herself off. She went and got her daughter and returned to the master suite to sit on Logan's wide bed with her.

Lifting her breast free of her robe, Lacey brushed the side of Rosie's tiny mouth with the nipple. Unerringly, that mouth found what it sought. Rosie latched on.

It didn't even hurt anymore, as it had the first few days. Now, there was only a pleasant tugging sensation and a sweet feeling of warmth and fullness as her milk came down and began to flow. Lacey smiled and whispered to her daughter, stroking the soft, bumpy head, which already seemed to have lost its pointiness and smoothed out into the shape of a very average-looking baby's head.

As Rosie settled into the rhythm of feeding, Lacey scooted back up against the headboard. She stared around her at the rich, deep textures of the bed linens, at the burled walnut bureau and bedside tables, at the royal blue walls and creamy white ceiling.

It was a very masculine room. Not a ruffle or a frill in sight. It didn't look like Jenna.

It looked like Logan.

And the rest of the house?

"You know what?" Lacey said aloud, stroking her daughter's head some more. "During this day of *un*reality checks, it has slowly become clear to me that I like it here. And I could live here quite comfortably."

The only rooms she'd want to change were Rosie's room and the room she'd choose for her studio.

Yes, the house bore Jenna's touch. But it was a very light, very loving touch. And really, Lacey was finding that seeing her sister's touch everywhere bothered her less and less with each hour that passed.

Perhaps, Lacey thought with a grin, it was because she had made her own mark here. A much more elemental mark than Jenna's.

Lacey had raided that big Sub-Zero refrigerator downstairs, in the middle of a warm September night, after she and Logan had spent hours making love. He'd hoisted her up on the cool green marble counter and made love to her again.

And here, in this bedroom—she had absolutely wonderful memories of what had happened here. If she closed her eyes and let her imagination take her, she could almost hear their sighs, their moans, their low, lazy laughter.

It *had* been a good time, those brief days in September. A beautiful time. A perfect, magical time. And at the end of it, she'd discovered that she'd found her love.

And now she was back here. In her hometown. Logan's wife.

*Un*reality check?

Maybe.

A big change, definitely. Major adjustments to be made, no doubt about that.

But she had her love. And her little girl.

A roof over their heads, food on the table. A room to work in, when she was ready to paint again.

It was a lot. And she was grateful for it.

"We're going to do fine, Rosie," she whispered to her daughter. "We are going to do just fine."

After they discussed the party, there were a number of other issues the partners decided they might as well deal with as long as they had each other's attention. Logan didn't sign for the check until after eleven.

And he didn't pull into his driveway until half an hour after that. The light in the master suite, which faced the street, was still on, a golden glow in the velvety darkness of the summer night. Logan stopped in the driveway as the garage door was rolling open. He stared up at the spill of warmth and brightness and felt something painfully sweet wash through him.

Urgency followed.

To be in there, where she was. To crawl into bed with her and turn off the light and...

He dragged in a breath. It didn't really matter what happened next. They might just drop off to sleep until Rosie woke them. Or Lacey might decide to show him how *helpful* she could be.

Then again, maybe she was angry with him by now.

He frowned. It *had* been—he glanced at his Rolex—almost ten hours since he'd dropped her off and headed for the office. He hadn't planned to be gone quite this long. Not on their first day home.

He'd also kept meaning to call her, just to check on her, to see how she and Rosie were doing. But every time he reached for the phone, something always cropped up that had to be dealt with right then. Somehow, he'd never gotten around to calling home.

Home.

Strange. He'd never thought of the house that way before.

It had always been just that. The house. *His* house. A place to live. An expensive, attractive possession of which he was justifiably proud.

But now...

Now, it had Lacey in it. And Rosie.

Now it had his *family* in it.

And somehow, that made all the difference.

Logan blinked and realized he was sitting in the driveway, the Cadillac's big engine purring softly in his ear. The garage door was all the way up and had been for over a minute now.

He hit the gas and shot into the garage so fast that he had to slam on the brakes to keep from hitting the far wall. The tires squealed and the car bounced on its cushion of shocks. He punched the button hooked to his visor and the garage door went rumbling down. Jumping from the car and slamming the door behind him, he entered the house through the laundry room door and jogged through the dark family room and breakfast room, headed straight for the front foyer and the stairs to the upper floor.

Lacey had put Rosie back in her crib at a little after eleven. She'd found a novel in a hall bookcase and settled back into bed to read.

Not too long after that, faintly, she heard a car pull up outside.

Logan.

She set her book aside, heard a low rumble—the garage door going up. After a minute or two, she heard a faint squealing sound—as if he'd hit the gas too hard and had to stop too fast. The garage door rumbled down again.

She sat forward, straining to hear. There it was. The door to the laundry room closing.

And then, seconds later, footsteps moving fast up the stairs. There was a certain urgency to them. As if he couldn't wait.

Couldn't wait to get to *her*....

He appeared in the doorway, hesitated there, seeking, then finding her, hope and tenderness and a kind of dark joy suffusing his features, burning in his eyes.

She thought, Why, Jenna was right.

He loves me.

He loves me in his actions. And he also loves me deep in his most secret heart.

And that, the love deep in his heart, he doesn't even know about.

"I'm sorry I'm so late." His voice was low, a little rough.

It's all right, she thought. But her throat felt so tight, the words wouldn't quite come.

So she smiled to show him he didn't need to worry. It was a shy, quivery sort of smile. Her heart was beating very fast, as if she'd run a long, hard race, one she'd known that she would lose—and reached the finish line to find herself victorious.

"You're not angry," he whispered. It seemed to mean the world to him.

She shook her head and felt her smile bloom wider on her mouth.

He swore, a passionate oath. And then he came to her.

She held out her arms to take him in.

Chapter 10

Four weeks and two days later, at ten in the morning on the thirteenth of August, Lacey got a clean bill of health from Dr. Enright, the obstetrician Logan had recommended.

The doctor fitted her for a new diaphragm and told her to feel free to resume sexual relations with her husband. Lacey smiled to herself. She and Logan had been having "sexual relations" all along, thank you. They'd made love in just about every way but one.

Now they could do that, too.

Lacey winked at the doctor. "Well, Doc. Looks like Friday the Thirteenth is my lucky day."

"Get that diaphragm first," Dr. Enright advised. "Give your body a little rest before the next baby."

From her carrier in the corner of the examining room, Rosie let out a happy gurgle. Lacey smiled at the sound. She did love her baby. And she wanted another. And another. And another after that. And so did Logan. But the doctor was right. No need to rush it.

She stopped in at the pharmacy on her way home to fill the prescription for her new diaphragm. After that, she visited a little deli she and Logan liked. She got dark bread and roast beef sliced paper-thin, and pastrami and a loaf of rye. And horseradish and fat dill pickles, too.

The twins were coming for lunch. She had talked to both Mira and Maud by phone since she'd moved back to town, but she hadn't invited them over until now. They had been thoroughly stunned when she'd told them that she'd married Logan Severance—and, as Lacey had expected, neither of them had approved of the match.

"You *married* him?" Mira had cried. "I can't believe it. You and Dr. Do-Right? Uh-uh. I mean, I know it was hot and heavy with you two back in September. And I can see why you might want to keep the baby. But *marriage.* To *him?* Did you have to go that far?"

Lacey had tried not to let Mira's reaction upset her. She'd explained calmly that she loved Logan and she believed he cared deeply for her in return. She was happy. Things were working out fine.

Mira had scoffed. "Ex-squeeze me. What is this? Bizarre." She warbled out a few bars of something that sounded like the theme from *The Twilight Zone.* "It's straight out of *The Stepford Wives,* if you ask me."

Lacey gritted her teeth. "Oh. Now I'm something out of a horror movie, a soulless clone of my former self? Thanks a bunch, Mir."

Mira backed off. A little. "Look. I'm sorry. It's just… whoa. I'm blown away. I haven't heard from you in months and then—"

"What's that got to do with anything? There have been lots of times when we haven't talked for months."

"You know what I mean. It's a shock. You call me up out of nowhere and say you've had a baby and married your sister's ex. It's a lot to take in."

"Well, deal with it. I went through some big changes myself over this."

"No kidding."

"It's the right thing for me. Mira, I love the man."

"Are you working?"

Leave it to Mira, Lacey thought. Mira knew right where to slide in the knife. "I just had a baby, remember?"

"You're not working."

"I'm fixing up a room. For my studio."

"But you're not working."

"I will be. Soon."

Mira demanded, "What does Xavier have to say about this?"

Xavier Hockland was a professional artist, a well-known and highly respected one. His shows always sold out. He worked in oils, for the most part. Like Lacey. And he had been her teacher and mentor until several months before—when he had learned she was pregnant and told her she had to make a choice: her baby or her art.

"Xavier is out of the picture," Lacey said.

"Why?"

"He just is, that's all. I don't want to talk about him."

"Fine. What about Barnaby, then? And Adele?" Barnaby and Adele were also artists, and friends of Lacey's in L.A. Barnaby rented a huge loft downtown, where he was storing a number of Lacey's paintings for her.

"I called them both," Lacey told Mira defiantly, "a couple of days ago. They congratulated me and wished me well."

"They don't know Logan Severance."

"What is that supposed to mean?"

Mira was silent, a silence that spoke volumes. After the quiet hummed through the line for several long seconds, she deigned to speak again. "I could become very worried about you, you know?"

Mentally, Lacey counted to ten. Then she suggested, "We'd better talk about you. How's the band doing?"

The band was the twins' passion and had been for over a decade. Mira played lead guitar and Maud played drums. They also had a bass player and a guy on keyboard. But the band really *belonged* to Mira and Maud. It had gone through a series of name changes over the years. The last Lacey had heard, they were calling it Mirror Image.

"You're switching subjects on me," Mira accused.

"You're right. I am. How's the band doing?"

Mira hesitated, but then let out a big sigh and answered Lacey's question. "We've been playing the Eureka Lounge Friday nights for a couple of months now."

"Hey. Way to go."

"But you know how it is. Maud has her job at the GiantValue Mart, Sunday through Thursday, as always.

Eight to four. And I'm still waiting tables four nights a week."

"What? Is that whining I hear?"

Mira chuckled. "Maybe what *I* need is a rich husband."

"Was that a dig?"

Mira laughed "Sure sounded like one, didn't it? Do you think I'm just jealous?"

"You? No way. You're not the jealous type."

"God, Lace. I can't believe you married him."

"Well, I did. Get used to it."

"I'm working on it."

They had talked for several minutes more. And when they hung up, it was on a reasonably cordial note. Lacey had called Maud right afterwards, figuring that she might as well get it over with.

Maud took the news in the same manner as her identical twin—only more so. She was shocked. Amazed. Blown away. And not the least bit pleased to learn that one of her best friends had "sold out" and married "Mr. Super-Straight Upwardly Mobile Big Shot M.D."

"He was fine for Jenna," Maud said. "And at least he always treated *her* with respect. But you know how he's been with you, Lace, all these years. How could you forget? Always after you, always telling you how to live your life, acting as if your career as an artist was just a big waste of time, some foolish, silly dream. How could you have…"

There was more in that vein. Finally, Lacey had been forced to lay down the law.

"He's my husband now, Maud. You are my friend

and I'll always love you. But if you keep talking against him, I can't deal with you anymore."

Maud had hung up on her.

And then called back a week later to apologize. They'd talked a couple of times since then. And yesterday, on the spur of the moment, Lacey had invited Maud over for lunch, then called Mira right afterward and asked her to come, too.

As she put the pastrami and roast beef into the meat drawer of the refrigerator, she muttered to herself, "Please. Don't let this visit be a total disaster."

It wasn't.

There *were* a number of potentially rocky moments, but Lacey had made up her mind ahead of time not to let the twins get to her.

Of course, they couldn't resist making cracks about the house.

"Straight out of *Better Homes and Gardens*," Mira said. "Totally *not* you, Lace."

Lacey had only smiled. "I like it. Jenna did most of it and I love my sister's taste."

"*Très* weird," said Maud. "Shouldn't you be, like, bothered, just a little, that she was his ex and she did the decorating?"

"Maybe I should. But I'm not."

"And just what does your big sister think of all this, anyway?"

"All what?"

"Come on. You know. You and Dr. Do-Right. Married. With a baby."

"She's happy for us. In fact, she thought I should marry him."

"Too strange."

"And she sent a complete layette for Rosie." The layette had arrived two days after they'd returned to Meadow Valley. Lacey had called and thanked her sister.

Jenna had called twice since then. But Lacey had cut both calls short. Once, because Rosie had demanded attention. And the second time, because Lacey had heard Logan's car pulling up in the driveway. She'd told her sister, "Logan's home. Gotta go."

Jenna had said, "Call me."

And Lacey had promised she'd do just that.

They hadn't spoken since, though, and that had been over three weeks ago.

"Anybody in there?" It was Maud.

Lacey laughed. "Sorry. Just thinking."

Maud grunted. "This is all pretty strange and unusual, if you ask me."

Mira muttered, "Bi-zarre." Then she shrugged. "But then again, Dr. Do-Right is one good-lookin' dude. And I gotta admit, I can relate to that fridge and the stove. Only the best, huh?"

"Right," Lacey agreed easily. "Only the best."

They did admire her studio, which she had fixed up just as she'd planned, with bare floors and white walls and rice-paper blinds.

"Now, *this* is you," said Maud. Her full red lips turned down at the corners. "It looks awfully...perfect, though. No clutter, no globs of paint on the worktable, no brushes soaking in jars. Have you been using it?"

She hadn't. And it was starting to bother her just a little. "I'm getting there."

Maud and Mira exchanged a glance, but before they could start in on her, the baby monitor Lacey had carried with her as she gave the twins the tour began emitting fussy little cries.

"She's awake." Mira's big dark eyes were gleaming. "I can't wait to meet her."

"And speaking of little darlings…" Lacey switched off the monitor and turned to Maud "…I thought you'd bring Devon." Devon was Maud's two-year-old. "I haven't seen him since last September. He was barely walking then."

"He's into everything now," Maud said. "And talking? You can't shut that kid up."

"Where is he?"

"Deke's got him." Deke and Maud had married right out of high school. Everyone had predicted that it would never last, but they were still going strong. "Deke's got Fridays off now, and he actually volunteered to babysit. I didn't argue. My mama didn't raise no fool."

"Bring Devon next time?"

Maud shrugged. "Sure."

Lacey led them to the baby's room, which now contained everything the discerning infant could desire, including a crib with a music-playing mobile above it and a double bureau appliquéd with balloons and teddy bears. The changing table had open shelves above it, so the diapers and receiving blankets were right within reach. The curtains and bedding sported clouds and rainbows on a sky-blue background.

"Wow," said Mira. "*This* is way cool." She was looking up at the ceiling, which Lacey had painted deep blue and decorated with a whole universe of planets, bright stars and silvery moons.

"So you *have* been painting," Maud teased, as Lacey picked up the fussing baby.

"You bet."

Mira turned her attention to the baby. "This girl is gorgeous. Let me hold her."

"Me, too," said Maud.

The twins passed the baby between them, each cuddling and cooing to her and calling her adorable. Then Lacey sat in the rocker to feed her. Finally, after a quick diaper change, they went downstairs. The twins took turns holding Rosie as Lacey got out the deli meats and breads.

Then they all made their own sandwiches. The twins had two each, roast beef *and* pastrami. They'd always loved to eat. Their lush, size-twelve figures attested to that fact.

"Umm," groaned Mira, as she bit into a fat dill pickle. "Heaven." She frowned at Lacey. "What? The nursing mother is only having one sandwich? Is this wise?"

Lacey patted her stomach, which had endured an endless number of crunches in the last few weeks. "I've lost most of what I gained with Rosie. Five pounds to go and I'll be back to my starting weight."

Mira crunched her pickle. "You only live once is what I always say."

"Exactly." Lacey grinned to herself, thinking of the night to come. Friday the Thirteenth, her lucky night.

"Eeeuu," cried Maud. "I know that look."

Lacey widened her eyes. "What look?"

"Sex look. So weird. You and Dr. Perfect really have a thing, huh?"

Lacey only smiled.

Mira bit into her pastrami on rye and chewed with lusty enthusiasm. She swallowed. "The world never changes. Opposites go on attracting."

Maud waved her pickle. "Just paint," she commanded. "Get up there in that big white room and paint."

Lacey said, "I will," and told herself that she meant it.

Logan came home at a little after eight.

It was perfect timing, really. Lacey had dinner all ready: herbed roast chicken, bow-tie pasta with olive oil and basil, and a salad of romaine, watercress and radicchio. Rosie had been fed and changed and put to bed.

Lacey was just getting out of the shower, humming to herself, feeling school-girl giddy and a little bit foolish, sighing at the thought of what was going to happen in the next few hours—if Logan didn't get held up by some emergency, of course.

There was always that possibility. But oh, she did hope there'd be no emergencies tonight.

She finished drying herself and pulled on the white silk robe that Logan had bought her a few weeks before. She liked to think of him, stopping in at that lingerie shop over on Commercial Street with the idea of buying some little wisp of nothing for her. She liked to picture him consulting with the saleswoman, describing her:

"She's blond, about this tall…" She liked to imagine him touching the satins and the laces with those fine big hands.

And she also liked the feel of the silk against her bare skin, that slinky, shivery, flowing feeling as it clung to her body, caressing each curve. She tied the sash around her waist and turned to the mirror over the black marble sink.

A big tortoiseshell clip held up her hair. She reached behind her and unsnapped it. Her hair spilled down her back. She shook her head, set the clip on the marble counter and reached up to comb her fingers through the heavy coiling strands.

That was when she caught sight of him.

He stood in the doorway to the bedroom, his tie hanging loose and the cuffs of his white dress shirt rolled to just below the elbows. He'd already gotten rid of his jacket, probably tossed it on the bed, or across a chair in the other room. He'd undone the top button of his shirt. She saw the shadow of his evening beard on his square jaw, and a hint of dark chest hair, in the V of his collar.

She met his eyes. Her heart caught, stuttered beneath her breastbone, then began beating slow and very hard, as if her blood had thickened somehow and it took a stronger, deeper beat to push it through her veins.

He raised a dark brow. "Well?"

She turned to face him, leaning back against the marble counter, gripping it with her hands, feeling that sweet loosening all through her, a warmth that pooled in her center and spread out from there. "I love it when you come home. Did I ever tell you that?"

Could those dark eyes of his get any darker? They seemed to, right then. "I thought maybe you'd call today, tell me how it went with Dr. Enright."

"I didn't want to bother you."

His mouth curled up on one side, a half smile, both ironic and tender. "You wanted me to wonder, to think about tonight."

"Well, maybe I did—a little, anyway. And I wanted to tell you in person."

"To tell me what?"

She slowly untied the sash of the robe. His eyes grew darker still.

She let the sash drop to the floor. The silk fell open.

He leaned in the doorway, folding his arms over his broad chest.

She touched her fingers to her collarbone, then traced a path downward, following the open facings of the robe, her fingers gliding between her breasts, over her stomach, lower still. When she reached her thighs, she let her hands fall to her sides and whispered, "Dr. Enright says I'm fine."

"Fine?" His eyes were dark as midnight now. "That means fully recovered?"

"That's right. Ready for anything…for everything…."

He went on watching, his gaze a brand, as she lifted her hands again to grasp the facings of the robe.

He was already striding toward her when she let the robe drop to the floor.

Chapter 11

When he reached her, he wrapped his arms around her and pulled her close. She sighed, reveling in the feel of him, the heat of him, the strength in his hands splayed on her bare back. She rubbed her cheek against his shoulder, breathing in the scent of him, which she could never put words to, but which she would have known anywhere.

She closed her eyes as he bent his head and pressed his lips to her throat. He drew on the skin.

She moaned, and then grasped his arms enough to pull away from the suckling kiss. "Stop that. You know if you put a mark there, it'll show."

He laughed, a husky, hungry laugh that set all her nerves humming. Then he pulled her close again and breathed against the reddened spot. "You like it."

She sighed some more. "I do. But remember that party Fiona Connery's giving us…"

He swore. "Tomorrow night."

She whispered in his ear, "We want them all to know we're happy, but…"

He laughed again, and lightly nipped the forbidden spot. "But not *that* happy."

"Exactly. So watch it."

"All right." He nuzzled lower, latched on to her left breast just above the nipple. She pulled him closer, moaned without shame, giving in to the kiss that marked her. Her milk flowed a little, wetting his shirt. Logan didn't mind.

He pulled back, studied his handiwork and then whispered gruffly, "There. No one will see. Now, come on."

She gave a glad cry as he scooped her up, one hand at her back and one under her knees, raising her high against his chest. He turned for their bedroom.

She clung to him, lifting her mouth to his. They kissed all the way to the bed.

He laid her down carefully, resting his hand on her belly for a moment, then sliding it down. He dipped a finger into the nest of dark gold curls at the juncture of her thighs. She closed her eyes, moaned deep in her throat and opened for him.

He stroked her, slowly, tenderly. She moved, unashamed, lifting herself toward his caress. After a moment, he slid that finger inside. She lifted herself higher still, and with an eager cry tried to reach for him.

But he stepped back. With a moan of disappointment, she opened her eyes to find that he hadn't really left her. He was only pulling off his tie, tossing it on a chair, and then getting rid of his shoes and his socks.

Barefoot, he came to her again, to the edge of the bed. She rose to her knees and began working at the buttons of his shirt, her fingers quick and eager, pressing herself close to him, kissing a path down his chest as each button gave way.

She pushed the shirt off his shoulders, tossed it aside. He was already unhooking his belt. She took care of the hooks at the waistband of his slacks and then pulled the zipper down in one slow sizzle of sound. Together, they pushed the slacks away. He stepped out of them, and his briefs as well.

She took his arm. "Come here. Come here to me...."

They fell across the bed together, legs in a tangle, mouths fusing, tongues playing. She wrapped her legs around him and felt him at her entrance.

Right then, she remembered. She stiffened.

He pulled back, looked down at her. "What?"

She lifted up, kissed his beard-roughened jaw. "You know I want more babies..."

He kissed her in return, but on the mouth, biting her lip a little. "It's too soon, I know."

The kisses always felt so good, so right, so wonderful.

His mouth closed over hers. She let him have her tongue, tasted the inside of his mouth, so slick and wet and lovely. And then he did the same to her, his tongue entering, sweeping the moist surfaces, retreating only to enter again.

Sometimes, when he was kissing her, she wondered

how she had lived without the taste of him. How she had gone all those years, knowing him, often irritated or even angry with him, and somehow managing never to realize that her anger and irritation only masked her own hunger. They were desire denied.

He touched her again, his hand finding her, parting her, stroking her, delving in.

She gasped. "I should...I have..."

His hand moved faster.

She gave herself up to it, her body gathering, rising. His kiss deepened. She cried into his mouth. He drank that cry as fulfillment shimmered through her.

Sometime later, she rose from the bed. "I'll be right back," she promised.

He made a low noise, part regret at her leaving him, however briefly, and part acquiescence to the necessity that she go.

He caught her hand, pressed his lips to it.

She pulled away with reluctance. "I promise. Right back."

In the bathroom, she took out her new diaphragm, spread on the contraceptive cream and, after only two tries, slid it into place. She rinsed her hands and returned to the bedroom.

He was waiting for her, sitting up on the edge of the bed. He held out his hand. She went to him. He guided her onto his lap. She hooked her legs around him, crying out when he filled her, then letting her head fall back, awash in the wonder of once again being joined to him.

For a time, they didn't move, except for the slow,

measured care of each breath. And then they couldn't help themselves. He raised his hips, pushing deeper as she pressed down.

And soon enough they fell together across the tangle of bedcovers. She rode him, moaning. He clutched her hips and pushed in hard. Then they were rolling, so he was on top. He braced his arms to either side of her and lifted his broad chest up, at the same time pressing in deeper down below. His eyes burned into hers.

"My love," she whispered. "Oh, yes, my love...."

He whispered something in return. It might have been her name.

And then there were no words. Only the two of them, only heat and desire and the pulse of fulfillment, starting at the point of joining and moving out, singing along every nerve, until they shuddered together and cried out as one.

The food was a little bit dry by the time they sat down to eat, both of them in their robes, at the dining room table, by candlelight. Logan had no complaints, though. He told her it was the best dry chicken he'd ever tasted. He opened a bottle of Pinot Grigio and Lacey allowed herself a half a glass, enough to raise and clink against his. They didn't need words for the toast. Their eyes said it all.

Lacey had taken exactly three bites and one sip of wine when the fussing started, little cries and bleats issuing from the monitor she had brought downstairs and parked on the sideboard.

She and Logan looked at each other and sighed.

"Could be worse," she said. "She could have decided she was hungry half an hour ago."

Lacey got up, gave her husband a kiss, and went to take care of their baby.

It was early, a little before ten, when she and Logan settled into bed again. She cuddled up close to him.

He smoothed her hair off her cheek and kissed her—a warm, chaste, peck of a kiss. "You make me so happy, Lacey Severance."

She dropped off to sleep smiling.

And woke in the middle of the night with an idea.

She turned toward her husband. Sound asleep. Good. And the monitor on the nightstand stood blessedly silent.

She slid from the bed with the stealth of a thief, careful to disturb the covers as little as possible. Once she was on her feet, she crept to the bathroom and got her robe. She stopped by the bed again, just long enough to get the baby monitor—or that had been her intent.

But somehow, she found herself hesitating there, wanting to bend across the bed, press her lips against Logan's temple, breathe in the warm, delicious scent of his skin.

And more than a kiss, she was tempted to crawl back in beside him. She would cuddle up close and rub her foot along his calf, her hand up his arm, over the strong muscles of his shoulder, onto his powerful chest with its mat of dark, curling hair.

She loved that, waking him in the middle of the night with caresses, loved the low sounds he made, his warm, sleepy kisses, the way he would…

No.

She was going to her studio and she was going right now.

She scooped up the monitor and tiptoed toward the hall.

She worked for an hour, lining out quick, rough sketches in pencil. Of Mira and Maud mostly, sitting at the kitchen table, Maud waving her pickle, Mira taking that first lusty bite of her pastrami sandwich.

It felt good to be working again.

The twins were right. She needed to make time for this, she needed to get in here on a regular basis, just an hour or two a day for right now, kind of ease into it gradually, slowly get herself back up to speed.

At a little before three, Rosie started crying. Lacey put her sketch pad aside, grabbed the monitor and turned off the lights.

When she got to the baby's room, she found Logan already there. He stood over the crib, his back to the door. Lacey paused at the threshold, warmth spreading through her. He'd pulled on a pair of pajama bottoms, but left his torso bare. As he bent over the crib, moon-light streaming in the window etched each muscle in silvery relief.

He lifted Rosie from her nest of blankets, raised her to his bare, beautifully formed shoulder and rubbed her tiny back, whispering, "Hey, there. It's okay. Daddy's here…"

He turned. Through the darkness, their eyes met.

Lacey moved into the room, setting the monitor on the bureau as she went by. "Here. I'll take her."

Logan passed her the squalling bundle. She carried the baby to the changing table to check her diaper. "Dry. Must be hungry."

Settling herself and the baby in the rocker, Lacey pushed the facing of her robe out of the way and cradled her breast, holding the nipple ready. Rosie latched right on and went to work.

"Where were you?" Logan was standing over her.

She looked up, gave him a smile. "In my studio. Sketching out a few ideas."

"At three in the morning?"

She'd been rocking slowly. Now she toed the floor and stopped the gentle movement of the chair. Something in his voice bothered her. Something…disapproving. Something that reminded her way too much of the Logan she had grown up telling herself she despised.

"Yes," she said levelly. "I was working in my studio. At three in the morning."

He was silent for a moment, staring down at her, his eyes gleaming through the shadows. She felt his possessiveness of her as a physical presence right then. That possessiveness aroused her. He wanted her so much, he didn't want to share her, except perhaps with their child.

A dark thrill coursed through her, to think that his need for her was that strong.

At the same time, she knew his possessiveness could pose a threat to them both, to what they had as a couple, to the life they were working together to build.

"Did those friends of yours come by today?" It almost sounded like an accusation.

"Yes," Lacey said. "Mira and Maud were here for

lunch. You have a problem with my friends paying me a visit?"

He shrugged, the movement casual, his expression anything but. "It's interesting, that's all. Those two come for lunch—and all of a sudden, you're up at three in the morning."

"Working," she said, stressing the word. "In my studio."

"You should get your rest when you can." His voice was low, soft—and yet she heard the command in it.

She decided it would be wisest to go straight for the throat about this. "I love you, Logan. But I won't be owned by you."

His eyes didn't waver. Still, she saw the flicker of unwilling understanding in their depths. He put his hand on the rocker back, holding it still. If she had tried to rock right then, she most likely would not have been able to.

She drew in a breath, closed her eyes briefly, focused on the physical, the warm wonder of her baby drawing on her breast, the feel of the silk robe he had given her, pleasurable as a lover's caress against her skin.

"I do love you," she whispered, gently now. "You don't *need* to own me."

Logan stared down at his wife's upturned face, wanting her, hard with the need for her, though at least she couldn't see that. The chair hid it from her view.

Lately, it had occurred to him that he had everything a man could ever ask for now. His wife. His daughter. A family that made his fine house a home.

And more. He had the nights.

With a woman who wanted him as much as he wanted her.

Sometimes, he thought of how empty it had all been before. An emptiness he hadn't even seen for what it was.

Always, there had been that emptiness. His mother had died when he was so young. His father, Dr. Logan Severance Sr., a good man but a distant one, had been left to raise him alone. His father had pushed him to work hard, to be the best. And Logan hadn't minded being pushed. He had wanted, when he was very young, to please his father.

And as he grew older, he found he wanted to be the best for the sake of excellence itself. For the feeling of satisfaction it gave him to know that he'd done what he could, given his all to any task he'd taken on.

The first moment he laid eyes on Jenna he'd known she was the one for him. Pretty and sweet and bright and fun to be with, she'd wanted a big family. Well-mannered and dignified, she would make the perfect doctor's wife.

He had loved her. But she hadn't filled the emptiness. And it hadn't mattered, because he'd had no idea that anything was missing.

As if his life had been this grayness, this...predictable procession of days.

And now, there was...color.

Color, which to him equaled Lacey.

Lacey in a silk robe and nothing else, waiting for him at the end of a long working day, turning from the mirror in their bathroom, blue eyes soft and hungry, opening the robe, dropping it to the floor....

The uncomfortable truth was that sometimes, lately, he couldn't help wondering how long it would last.

She said that she loved him. He believed that she did. For now.

But she *was* Lacey. Impossible, unpredictable, incredible Lacey.

He *could* lose her.

So easily. Maybe not to another man. For some reason, he didn't fear that kind of rival.

But to her stubborn dream of a life as an artist. Yes. That damn dream could very well take her away from him.

"Logan..." She was still looking up at him, waiting for him to speak, to say the reasonable thing.

He let go of the chair. "I woke up and you weren't there. I got worried, that's all."

"It's important to me, to start getting back to work. Rosie makes her demands. And you know I want to be there for you, when you get home. But any time neither of you needs me, and I get the urge to pay a visit to my studio..." She let the thought finish itself.

He nodded, said the words she needed to hear, the fair words, the reasonable ones. "Of course. I understand."

She smiled, and his heart did something physically impossible inside his chest. "All right, then," she whispered.

Rosie let out a small, sweet sigh. Her little eyes were shut. She'd stopped nursing. Logan looked down at his sleeping daughter, at his wife's breast, the just-released nipple shining and taut. "Come back to bed," he said, and knew that his longing was there in his voice.

Lacey nodded, answered huskily, "Yes. In a few minutes. I should at least try her on the other side first."

So he waited there with her in the dark as she put his daughter to her other breast. Rosie woke enough to begin nursing again. But in three or four minutes, her tiny mouth went loose once more.

"She's done." Lacey slid the robe back in place and lifted Rosie to her shoulder. Next, there was the diaper to change. And then finally, Lacey put the baby in the crib and tucked the blankets around her.

"Come to bed."

She hung back. "Logan…"

"What?"

"I do love you. So very much. Please believe me."

He pulled her into his arms then, held the silk, the softness, the warmth of her close. She tipped up her head and he kissed her, a deep kiss, one that he broke only to whisper with more urgency than before, "To bed. Come on."

She went willingly then, pausing only to collect the baby monitor from the bureau as they went by.

Chapter 12

"It's so lovely to meet you at last," said Fiona Connery, reaching for Lacey's hand. "Where is the baby?"

"Rosie's at home," Lacey replied, "with a sitter."

"Ah. Well." Fiona twined her fingers with Lacey's in a proprietary fashion and swept out her other arm in a gesture that indicated the whole of her large, beautifully appointed house and each and every one of her well-dressed, well-off, well-behaved guests. "Probably a good idea. What fun would a one-and-a-half-month-old have at something like this?"

Lacey agreed. "Maybe next time—or better still, the time after that."

Fiona leaned close. She wore a subtle, expensive perfume, one that suited her—floral, with a hint of musk. "Now, I shall drag you around for a moment, showing you off." She captured Lacey's free hand, then pulled both hands wide and stepped back. "This is a gorgeous dress."

Lacey smiled—modestly, of course. The dress was a simple, just-above-the-knee black velvet sheath, sleeveless, with a scoop neck. She'd bought it a week ago, specifically for Fiona's party. It had been easy to choose. She'd simply imagined what her sister might wear to an event like this.

Fiona spoke to Logan, who stood behind Lacey. "Your wife has great taste."

"I think so, too."

Lacey cast a glance back at him. He looked sexy and protective. She wanted to grab him and press herself against him and whisper something thoroughly inappropriate in his ear.

But Fiona was already pulling her toward the wide arch that led to the living room. "Come on. You have to meet Daniel. And Helen—or have you already met Helen?"

"No, not yet."

"She's a dear. You'll love her." Fiona sent a reassuring smile over her shoulder in Logan's direction. "Don't worry. You'll have this lovely wife of yours back soon enough."

Logan waved them on their way.

The next few hours weren't bad at all. Lacey smiled and laughed and talked about her baby and how happy she and Logan were. When asked about her life before her marriage, she spoke briefly of her work as an artist—*very* briefly, as a matter of fact. No one seemed that interested in what she'd been doing with herself before she married Logan, and that was fine with her.

Her aim was to make a good impression, for Logan's sake. And she felt, as the evening progressed, that she was doing a pretty fair job of it.

She did have to turn down a couple of offers to get involved on charity committees. Fiona asked if she'd like to help out with Miner's General's Auxiliary. And the wife of a doctor who had his office in Logan's building wondered if Lacey might want to join Helping Hands, a group of doctors' wives who raised funds for such worthy causes as AIDS and breast cancer research.

She explained to both women that she would love to help out, but she couldn't right at the moment. She said she needed to get back to work in her studio before she took on anything else. With a new baby, and all the other changes that had taken place in her life lately, somehow there were just never enough hours in a day.

Fiona and the other woman smiled graciously and assured her that they understood. Lacey wasn't sure they did. And she felt just a little bit guilty at having to say no.

For about a minute and a half.

Then she reminded herself that she'd never claimed to be the ideal doctor's wife. She was an artist. After her family, her work had to come first—at least until she got herself back on track. And then, well, she'd see about taking on a little volunteer work.

It was just after eleven when she and Logan thanked their hostess for a terrific evening.

Fiona begged them to stay longer. "Don't go yet. The fun is only beginning."

Lacey put on an appropriately regretful expression.

"We'd love to stay. Unfortunately, Rosie will be waking up soon, if she hasn't already. She'll be hungry. And guess who has to be there to feed her?"

"Ah," said Fiona, "I don't want to let you go, but I do understand." She leaned forward and kissed Lacey on the cheek. "It is so good to meet you at last. And I want to see more of you. How about lunch next week? I could drop in at your house, just long enough to meet little Rosie. Perhaps then…you *do* have a sitter you can call?"

"Well, I—"

Fiona ran right on. "I was thinking that we could get out for an hour or two, just you and I, that we could really get a chance to put our heads together. How would that be?"

Put our heads together about what? Lacey wondered.

Logan said, "Mrs. Hopper can watch the baby for a couple of hours, don't you think, Lacey?"

The housekeeper, who came twice a week, probably could watch Rosie—and no doubt would quite willingly. Mrs. Hopper loved babies. And Lacey always paid her extra whenever she agreed to baby-sit for an hour or two while Lacey ran errands.

Fiona pressed on. "How about a week from this coming Wednesday? That should give you plenty of time to work things out with a sitter. Say right around noonish?"

Lacey felt slightly railroaded, but then wondered why. It *was* only lunch. Wasn't it?

Logan and Fiona were waiting to hear her reply.

She put on her most gracious smile and said she'd love to join Fiona for lunch. And a week from Wednesday would be fine.

* * *

The twins came to visit again on Friday. Maud brought her little boy, Devon.

Lacey exclaimed over how much he'd grown.

She was also able to inform the twins that she'd spent several hours in her studio since their last visit.

"I have no big projects in the works yet, but I have a lot of ideas. I've been drawing again. It's slowly coming back to me."

"Way to go, Lace," cheered Mira.

Maud agreed, "We're proud of you. Keep it up."

They asked her when she'd be coming to the Eureka Lounge to hear the band again. "It's August," Maud reminded her. "Almost a year since the last time you heard us play. We've been adding in a few of those great old blues and soul classics to some of our sets, 'Stormy Monday' and 'When a Man Loves a Woman.' Mira's doing lead vocals on them. And you know how she can wail."

Lacey said she'd try, but with the baby and with Logan's demanding schedule, it was always a challenge arranging a night out.

Maud made a face. "We didn't say you had to bring *him*."

"But I want to bring *him*," she replied. "I have high hopes that someday the three of you will learn to get along."

Mira groaned. "Gag me with a stethoscope—and don't hold your breath. He thinks we're a bad influence on you. He's *always* thought so. Remember back in high school, when we broke into the science lab before the advanced biology classes got their vivisection lesson and let all those poor doomed frogs out of their terrariums? He told your mother that she should forbid you to hang with us ever again."

"That was high school."

"You're trying to tell us he's changed his mind about us?"

Lacey coughed. "Well…"

"Don't try," Maud advised. "You'll only be lying and we won't believe it. Just come hear us play—and bring *him* if you have to."

Lacey said she would come—eventually.

The twins shared a significant glance and left it at that.

That evening, Lacey mentioned the idea to Logan. "They play on Friday nights, so I was thinking that maybe we could—"

He was shaking his head before she'd even finished making the suggestion. "I'm not much for heavy metal music, Lace."

She started to set him straight. "The twins' band isn't heavy metal…" But then she remembered that it had been at one time. "Well, maybe it *was.* Seven or eight years ago. They've changed a lot since then, though. I think you'd like them now."

He gave her one of his irritatingly superior doubtful looks and said that maybe, some evening, in a few weeks…

Wednesday, Fiona arrived right at noon. She held the baby and declared her "an absolute doll."

"Daniel and I have two of our own, did you know? Patrice and Daniel, Jr. Patrice is at Stanford. Daniel, Jr. is at UCLA. I miss them, but I do manage to keep busy." She laughed. "Do I ever. Being a doctor's wife is a full-time job."

And that, as it turned out, was the theme of Lacey's lunch date with Fiona: being a doctor's wife is a full-time job.

Fiona asked her again to join a couple of committees. Lacey said she just might do that. Later. Right now, as she'd already explained, she had her own work to catch up on.

Fiona accepted Lacey's refusal with a dazzling smile. "Don't expect me to stop asking you."

Lacey laughed. She really did like Fiona. "Fiona. You are not going to charm me into doing things your way."

Fiona put on a wide-eyed expression and splayed her beautifully manicured hand against her chest. "Me? Try to charm you? Never. You and Logan *will* make it to the Health Aid Society's annual banquet, won't you? It's on the fourth of September. Everyone turns out for it. Daniel and I will be there, of course. And Helen and her husband. It's important that the practice be well-represented."

Lacey was able to say yes to that one. "Logan mentioned the banquet. He told me he wanted to go. So when the invitation came, I went right ahead and sent in the check for two tickets."

Fiona beamed. "Good. I'm so glad." She reached across and patted Lacey's arm. "We'll make a proper doctor's wife out of you yet."

Lacey decided she was going to have to be more direct. She pushed her empty plate aside, rested her forearms on the table and leaned toward the woman across from her. "Fiona. Be honest. I'm sure you've heard about me."

Fiona sat back. She was blushing, a blush that looked thoroughly enchanting on her. "Well, now. What can I say when you put me on the spot like this? Meadow Valley has grown a lot in the past couple of decades. But at heart, it's still a small town, isn't it?"

"Yes, it is. And if you've asked around, you must have learned that I've never been a 'proper' anything."

Fiona waved a hand. "Oh, now. A childish prank or two…"

"I'm never going to try to be someone I'm not, Fiona. I love Logan and I'm proud to be his wife. But I am not Jenna. I'm me."

"I understand that. I do."

"Good. Then you and I will get along just fine."

Fiona sat forward again. "Of course we will—and you know, the Aid to the Indigent fall rummage sale is almost upon us. September eleventh and twelfth, can you believe it? If you could see your way clear to making a few calls next week to ask for donations, and then another set of reminder calls the week of the sale, just to let people know again that we do need their donations—"

"Fiona, don't you ever give up?"

"Never. What about those calls?"

Lacey shook her head—and said yes.

Fiona said, "Wonderful. And if you'd just agree to a few hours on Saturday the eleventh, manning a booth, well, I cannot tell you how grateful I would be."

Lacey suppressed a sigh. "Okay. I'll take a booth—

if you promise me that'll be all for a couple of months, at least."

"I promise."

"All right, then."

"Excellent—and where is our waitress? I want a fruit tart, just for a little extra treat."

"I think Fiona likes you," Logan said later, when Lacey told him about their lunch.

"Maybe she does," Lacey admitted. "She's also determined to show me the way to be a real asset to you and to the practice."

"Don't let her railroad you," he advised. "Just do what you want to do."

That pleased her. Fiona might hope to make her over into the perfect doctor's wife, but Logan didn't appear to be in on the scheme. She winked at him. "Have I ever done anything but exactly what I wanted to do?"

He laughed then. "Not that I can recall."

"I have an idea," she suggested brightly. "How about a visit to the Eureka Lounge this Friday night? You can hear Mira sing the blues."

His expression darkened. "What brought that up?"

"I'm learning from Fiona. When you want someone to do something, you have to ask them. Repeatedly, if necessary."

"I don't think I'm ready to hear Mira sing the blues—not this week, anyway."

"Why did I know you'd say that?"

"I haven't a clue."

"I'm not giving up."

"I'll consider that a warning."

"Please do."

He pulled her close and planted a kiss on the tip of her nose. "You have an extremely self-satisfied look on your face, Mrs. Severance."

"That's not self-satisfaction. That's contentment. All in all, even though I've yet to drag you to the Eureka Lounge, I'd still say this marriage of ours is working out pretty well."

"I couldn't agree with you more," he said, and kissed her again, this time on the mouth.

They went up to bed not long after that and made slow, delicious love. Lacey thought, as she dropped off to sleep a little later, that she'd never been happier. She had her love and her baby and little by little, she was getting back to work.

Xavier Hockland called the next day.

Chapter 13

"I got your number from Barnaby," Xavier said in that slightly bored, thoroughly arrogant tone Lacey remembered so well. "I asked him if I could just drop by his loft and show Belinda Goldstone the work you did last winter. He said I had to check with you first."

Belinda Goldstone. Lacey's pulse accelerated. Belinda Goldstone was one of L.A.'s premiere art dealers. She owned a gallery where she hung only the works of top contemporary artists.

"Lace. Are you there?"

Lacey swallowed. "I'm here."

"I heard you had that baby."

That baby. What was the matter with him? "Her name is Rosie."

"And you adore her." Xavier sighed.

"Yes, I do. She's one of the two best things that ever happened to me."

"The other being?"

"My husband, Logan."

Xavier said nothing. Lacey waited him out. Finally, he asked, "Have you done any work at all in the past few months?"

"Xavier. Let's not get started on that. What I'm working on, or when, or how much time I'm giving to it is no longer your concern. What's this about Belinda Goldstone?"

He let a few seconds elapse, just to show her he was controlling the conversation, before he said, "I had lunch with her yesterday. She asked about you."

Lacey was frowning. "I hardly know her. I've met her at two or three openings, that's all—just to shake her hand and say, 'How are you?' Why would she ask about me?"

Xavier sighed again. "Until you decided to throw it all away, you *were* my protégée."

Lacey knew that wasn't all of it. "Okay. So she asked about me. And you told her I'd thrown it all away. End of conversation."

Xavier made an impatient sound. "All right, all right. Word gets around. There has been some buzz about that series of figure studies you were working on before you took off to…complete your gestation period in the wilds of Wyoming."

"So she asked about the series I was working on last winter, is that it?"

"Yes."

"And you told her…?"

Another pause, then he gave out grudgingly, "That they were fabulous. Sensual. Arresting. Powerful. I laid on the adjectives. They were only the truth."

Lacey's heart had started pounding hard again. "And she asked if she could see them?"

"Yes. I told her I'd check into it. Will you call that damn Barnaby and tell him it's all right if I show them to her?"

Lacey resisted the urge to throw back her head and let out a long, loud yelp of glee.

"Lace? Will you call Barnaby?"

"Yes, Xavier, I will."

"Thank you."

"Thank *you*."

"You're welcome," Xavier said. "And there's one other thing…"

"Yes?"

"Perhaps I was a little out of line, about that baby."

"Her name is Rosie. And yes, you were out of line."

"You're happy."

"I am."

"And Barnaby said the man's a doctor. That he has money."

"What are you getting at, Xavier?"

"Happiness and money. These are good things for an artist. Some opt for struggle—they buy into the myth that suffering will somehow improve the work. This is delusional. Struggle only wears one down. The work gets done in spite of suffering, not because of it. A place to work, and few outside worries. That's what an artist needs. Happiness and money can help a lot in that regard. When you told me about the baby, I understood you were going to be dealing with it on your own. Now I can see that isn't the case, so perhaps I was too quick to offer my advice on the subject."

"Xavier, is this an apology?"

"I never apologize. I'm just pleased to hear you're doing well. Have Barnaby call me."

"Yes. Yes, I will."

At first, Lacey told no one about Xavier's call—except Barnaby in L.A. It was her little secret she kept just to herself.

Belinda Goldstone had asked to see her work.

It might mean nothing.

Or it might mean a great deal.

She wouldn't know until Xavier—or Belinda Goldstone herself—called back. *If* one of them called back.

Until then, well, she certainly did feel terrific about herself. She found it easier to concentrate when she went into her studio. Her confidence had just gotten a big boost, and that did wonders for her ability to focus when she worked.

And beyond progress in her work, it was pure self-indulgent delight just to fantasize a little about what this might mean. To imagine her paintings hanging in Belinda Goldstone's gallery.

In her fantasy, of course, the show would sell out before the opening. And her beautiful paintings of Logan would...

Logan.

That did give her pause. She had yet to tell him that there were nine nudes of him—his face carefully disguised, of course—stored in Barnaby Cole's L.A. loft.

She probably *should* have told him before now.

In fact, she realized, she couldn't afford to put off telling him any longer. If anything did come of Belinda Goldstone's visit to Barnaby's loft, she wanted her husband to be reasonably prepared. It only seemed fair that he should know about the existence of the paintings before she sprung the news that Belinda Goldstone wanted to hang them in her gallery.

She told him two nights after Xavier called, over a dinner of roast beef, baby carrots and new potatoes— a meal that was one of his favorites. She'd decided it wouldn't hurt to coddle him a little before she hit him with the information she probably shouldn't have kept from him in the first place.

He took the news amazingly well. He seemed surprised, but not offended. And he had a number of questions.

"You say it's impossible to tell that I was your…" He frowned, seeking the right word.

She provided one. "Inspiration?"

"Okay. I'll go with that. Will anyone be able to tell that I *inspired* you?"

"Well," she hedged. "People who know you might guess. But I promise, they won't know for certain. The face in each painting is hidden—with a mask, or by shadows, or because the figure is turned away from the viewer."

He was still frowning. "Exactly how nude is nude?"

"Logan. What is that supposed to mean?"

He tried again. "I guess I'm asking, are they…tasteful?"

She had to laugh. "*Tasteful* wasn't exactly what I was shooting for."

He set down his fork. "Let me put it this way. What shows?"

She understood. And laughed again. "How can such a sexy man be such a prude?"

"Just answer me. What shows?"

"No genitals. How's that?"

He picked up his fork again. "A relief."

They ate in silence for a minute or two. Then he said, "There are nine of them?"

"Uh-huh."

"How long did it take you to paint them?"

"I painted the first one here in Meadow Valley, when I was staying with Jenna, at the beginning of October."

He glowered at her. "Right after you sent me away."

She let the implied accusation pass and stuck to the issue. "Yes. And I finished the ninth one in L.A., in early April, about a month before I left for Wyoming."

He drank from his wineglass and set it down. His expression had softened. "I guess that means I was on your mind a lot, all those months."

"Yes, Logan, you were." She cut a bite of meat, concentrating on the small task, then glanced up through her lashes at him. "You know that you were."

His eyes were very dark. "You were on my mind, too."

"I'm glad." She waited, thinking, It's going to happen now. He's going to actually get the words out. He's going to say that he loves me.

But the moment passed. He watched her with desire,

with tenderness, with a hint of exasperation—and with what she knew to be love.

He just didn't say it.

"Why are you telling me now?" he asked quietly.

She poked the bite of meat into her mouth and chewed, thinking, *Well, what did I expect? The man is hardheaded, but he's certainly no fool.*

So what now? She could lie and keep her little secret to herself. He might never have to know.

But if Xavier or Belinda Goldstone *did* call...

So much for her secret.

She finished chewing. He waited, his eyes never leaving her face.

She swallowed. "You remember the artist I went to L.A. to study under? I think I talked about him a little, last September."

Logan thought for a minute. "Hockland, right? Xavier Hockland."

"Yes, Xavier Hockland. He called, the day before yesterday with some good news...or it *could* be good news."

Logan had set his fork down again, but he didn't speak. He was waiting for her to tell him whatever it was she had to say.

She sucked in a breath. "Xavier had lunch with a certain very well-known art dealer, Belinda Goldstone, a few days ago. She'd heard about the paintings—through the grapevine, you could say. She asked to see them. He wanted my permission to show them to her."

"Xavier Hockland has the paintings?"

"No, they're at Barnaby Cole's. I've told you about Barnaby, haven't I? He's a friend. He has a big loft.

Downtown. And Xavier wanted to take Belinda Goldstone there, to see them."

"And?"

"And I said yes, that it was fine with me if Xavier
showed her my paintings."

"What else?"

"Nothing else. Yet."

"A reputable art dealer wants to see some of your
paintings. You gave Xavier Hockland permission to
show them to her. And that's all."

"Yes," she said. "That's all. As of now. Naturally,
I'm hoping more will come of it."

"Like what?"

She realized she couldn't read him. He seemed distant. Or at least he had in the past few moments. Distant
and a little bit cold. Strange. She'd anticipated that he
might be distant and cold, even angry with her, when he
learned of the existence of the paintings. But she never
would have guessed that this other bit of news would
upset him.

"Logan. What's the matter?"

"Nothing. Just tell me. What exactly are you hoping
for?"

His disdainful tone grated. She answered with heat.
"What do you think I'm hoping for? That Belinda Goldstone will want to hang my paintings in her gallery, that
I'll have a major show and that the show will sell out.
What do we all hope for, Logan? Appreciation. Accep-
tance. To get paid and paid well for the work that we've
done."

He was sitting very still. "You're angry," he said.

She pushed her plate away. "No. Yes. It means a

lot to me, that's all, that someone like Belinda Gold-stone wants to see my work. I'd like to think that you're pleased for me. But you don't seem pleased. You don't seem pleased at all."

"I *am* pleased."

She stared at him across the table, wanting to believe him, but not quite able to.

He slid his napkin in at the side of his plate and pushed his chair back. "Lace..." His eyes pleaded. His tone was gentle again.

Her heart went to mush.

She let her shoulders droop. "I guess I am a little sensitive about this."

In two long strides he was beside her, taking her hand, pulling her up and into his waiting arms. "I'm sorry," he whispered as he stroked her hair. "I didn't mean to hurt you...."

She wrapped her arms around him, pressed herself close. "It's okay. Never mind. You're right. Nothing's really happened yet, anyway. And it could very well turn out that nothing will."

He tipped her chin up and his mouth came down to cover hers. With a low moan, she slid her arms around his neck.

A few minutes later, they went upstairs.

The next day was Sunday. Logan didn't have to work. They spent a long, lazy morning reading the Sunday papers in bed, with Rosie between them, gur-gling and cooing and waving her tiny, plump hands above the blankets.

Later, they dressed and put Rosie in her car seat and

drove down into the Valley to buy a few things for the house—some new deck chairs and an entry hall table. That night, they left Rosie with a sitter and went out to dinner at a place they both liked over on Commercial Street.

It wasn't until Monday morning after Logan had left for his office that Lacey found herself rethinking their exchange of Saturday night. As Rosie napped, she sat in her studio with her sketch pad in her lap and brooded over the words her husband hadn't said.

Simple expressions of encouragement and understanding, like...

Good luck.

Or, I'll keep my fingers crossed for you.

Or, Of course, Belinda Goldstone will call.

Or, You're a damn good artist and it's about time you got a break.

Eventually, Rosie woke. Lacey heard the fitful cries from the monitor on the windowsill and came back to herself with a start.

She looked down at the sketch pad in her hands.

Blank.

Well, she thought, *that's what brooding will get you. Nowhere.*

Was she overreacting?

Probably.

As she'd admitted to Logan the other night, she *was* sensitive on this subject. Probably way *too* sensitive.

The wisest thing to do, she knew, was to let it go for now. And when the subject came up again, she'd try her best to approach it calmly and rationally. She'd make a concerted effort not to allow her own insecurities to get all mixed up with whatever might be bothering her husband.

Rosie cried louder.

Lacey set her sketch pad aside and went to take care of her baby.

Two days later, on Wednesday, at eleven in the morning, Mack called from a Key West hospital.

"It's a boy," he announced. "Eight pounds, two ounces."

Lacey let out a glad cry. "Oh, Mack! Congratulations. I can hardly believe it. His name. What's his name?"

"Ian Alexander. The Alexander's for my stepfather—"

"And Ian after our dad. Great choice."

"We think so."

"Is Jenna…?"

"She's right here. A little tired."

"I'll bet. I promise I won't keep her long."

Jenna came on the line. "Lace. Hello."

Lacey's eyes blurred with sudden moisture. She swiped at them with the heel of her hand. "Hey. A beautiful boy, huh?"

"Yep. You're an auntie."

"Oh, Jen. I can't believe it. I…I want to see him."

"Then come. Bring Rosie. And Logan. Come see us."

"Oh, Jen. You know I'd love to…"

Both sisters were silent. Lacey knew that Jenna was thinking the same thing that she was.

Logan would find some reason why they couldn't go.

Jenna hitched in a tight little breath. "It's all right," she said, her voice weary. "I understand. Maybe someday…"

"Yes," Lacey agreed. "Someday soon…" Why did that feel like such a complete lie? "…and I should let you go now, shouldn't I?"

"I'll call you, in a day or two, after we're out of this hospital and back home where we belong."

"Yes. Oh, please do."

"We…we don't talk enough anymore, Lace."

Lacey closed her eyes and murmured, "I know."

"What? I can hardly hear you."

Lacey spoke right into the mouthpiece this time. "I said, I know. We don't talk enough. I keep meaning to call you, but…" But what? There was really no excuse.

Except that she and Logan had a good life. And Jenna wasn't part of it. Jenna was someone Lacey and Logan never talked about.

Logan certainly never mentioned her. He'd loved Jenna for over a decade, had wanted to marry her. She had helped to make his house a beautiful home. Yet it was as if he'd prefer to pretend that she simply didn't exist.

Then again, maybe Lacey had it wrong. Yes, Logan never mentioned Jenna. But Lacey never talked about her either.

Jenna said, "Let's not allow ourselves to drift apart."

Lacey brushed away more tears. "It's a deal."

"I love you."

"Oh, and I love you, too."

Jenna laughed then, a tired sound, but a cheerful one.

"My husband is grabbing the phone from me now. He seems to think I've talked long enough. I'll call…"

"Okay. Bye."

Mack came back on. "Think about it," he said. "Come for a visit. Talk it over with that husband of yours. I think it's about time we all started letting bygones be bygones."

It was good advice and Lacey knew it. "All right," she said.

"What was that?"

"I said, all right, Mack. I'll talk to him."

Chapter 14

That evening, Lacey told Logan that Jenna and Mack's baby had been born.

He said, "Be sure to congratulate them for me."

They were sitting in the family room, on the long sofa there. She toed off her shoes and folded her legs under her, to the side. "I thought I'd send them a baby swing. I love the one we got for Rosie. Keeps her happy for long stretches of time."

"A baby swing sounds good to me."

She leaned her head against his arm, which rested along the sofa back. Her heart was racing. But she kept her voice offhand. "Oh, and Jenna asked us to come to Key West. For a visit. Mack mentioned the idea, too."

She felt his bicep flex beneath her cheek. "Lace, I can't get away right now. Not so soon after a two-week trip to Wyoming."

She sat up straight and sought his eyes. "All right. Then when?"

He hesitated, but finally gave out reluctantly, "Maybe next spring."

In the spring. Six or seven months. That wouldn't be so bad, if she could get a definite commitment. "The spring then. In April? I'll tell Jenna when she calls."

He was already shaking his head. "Let's just wait until April and think about it then."

"But Logan—"

"I can't make any promises about seven months from now." His tone had cooled, and there was an underpinning of steel in it. "That's all there is to it."

Okay, Lacey thought. We've danced around this long enough. Now, we'd better get down to a little honesty on the subject. "Logan, what's the real problem here?"

"I told you. I can't—"

She didn't let him finish. "Is it that you still feel uncomfortable at the thought of seeing Jenna and Mack again?"

He didn't answer for a moment. Then he admitted, "Yes. The idea does make me uncomfortable. But Jenna is your sister. And I suppose we'll have to see her and McGarrity now and then."

"We'll *have* to see them?"

He looked at her levelly. "That's what I said. Please don't ask me to pretend it's something I'm looking forward to."

She stared right back at him, eye-to-eye. "I'm not asking you to pretend anything. I'm asking you to start thinking about putting all the old garbage behind you."

"Fine. I'll do that. To the best of my ability."

She let out a long breath. "To the best of your ability?"

"That's what I said."

She bit her lower lip, released it. "That's just great." She found she didn't want to sit there with him, not right then. She slid her feet to the rug and padded to the big window that looked out on the redwood deck. The outside lights were on, illuminating the new deck furniture they'd bought the other day, as well as the old willow tree that grew right next to the backyard steps. The willow's leaves were still summer-green. But soon enough, those leaves would begin to turn.

It was September again. In a few weeks, it would be a full year since she had knocked on his door, offering a shoulder to cry on and a four-layer devil's food cake.

A full year. In that time, she had learned that she loved him. She had borne his child. And she had come to believe that he loved her.

And was that the real problem here, the one she was trying to get them both to deal with?

She believed he loved her. But he had never said he did.

In some ways, it seemed that Jenna's gentle, loving spirit stood between them still. And never more so than now, when he refused to take the steps required to put old hurts away for good.

She heard him approach. He put his hands on her shoulders. She stiffened, but then made her body relax beneath his touch. She felt his breath, warm across the crown of her head. "Lace. Just give it a little more time, all right?"

"How much more time?"

He didn't answer, but his hands tightened a fraction on her shoulders, a signal that he wanted her to lean back against him.

She folded her arms over her stomach and remained fully upright. "Logan, you say you're happy with me."

"I am."

"Then why can't you let the past go? Why can't you forgive my sister for…choosing another man over you?" She turned beneath his hands, so she could face him. "I don't call her anymore, Logan. Because I feel uncomfortable myself, about the whole thing. I don't want it to be like this. I don't want to lose touch with her. She's my sister. And she's my friend. And I love her very much."

"I never said I expected you to cut off contact with her."

"No. But you…you don't want me to talk about her. You behave as if you'd just as soon forget that she and Mack even exist."

She paused, waiting for him to argue with her, to reassure her, to tell her he didn't mind talking about Jenna at all. That he most certainly did not want to forget she existed.

But he didn't argue.

She made her final point. "You won't go and visit her."

He did have a reply to that. "I will. Eventually. You just have to back off a little. Give me a little more time."

More time. "You already said that."

"And I think it's a reasonable request."

She stared at him, thinking, *I love you. Do you love me?*

Should she ask him?

Somehow, she just couldn't bear to.

It seemed to her that a declaration of love ought to be freely given. It wasn't something a woman should pull out of a man—like a splinter or a shameful confession.

She warned in a gentle voice, "Don't take too much time, Logan. Eventually I'll simply go to Key West without you."

"I understand," he said.

"Do you?"

"Let it go, Lace."

"All right. I will. For now."

Two days later, when Jenna called, Lacey told her it would be a while before she and Logan visited. Jenna didn't ask why. She said she'd look forward to their visit whenever it came. And that any time Lacey needed her, all she had to do was call.

The phone rang again not two minutes after Lacey hung up from her conversation with Jenna.

It was Barnaby Cole. "I had to call you. My fingers were just itching to punch up your number."

Lacey laughed, but her heart had started beating hard and fast. "What?"

"They just left."

"I take it you mean Xavier and Belinda Goldstone."

"You take it right." Barnaby's voice, always deep and booming, seemed even deeper than usual, and charged with excitement. Lacey could see him in her mind's eye, a chocolate-skinned, muscular giant of a man, hunched over the phone, fiddling with the small gold hoop he always wore in his left ear.

"How long were they there?" she demanded.

"Over an hour."

"And? What happened? Barnaby, stop torturing me. Tell me, before I have a heart attack."

"Tell you—?"

"Everything."

"Everything." He chuckled, that low, rolling chuckle of his that Lacey had always loved. "All right. Let's see. They came up the freight elevator, since that's the only way to get here. Xavier made the introductions. The art dealer said the same thing that everybody says. It must be fabulous to have all this space—but the neighborhood is so dangerous, didn't I worry a little about my own safety? I said—"

"Barnaby. Stop it."

He chuckled some more. "Stop what?"

"When I said 'everything,' you know what I meant."

He pretended innocence. "Oh. You want to hear about your *paintings...*."

"That's right. So tell me. Tell me right now."

"Well, let's see. I'd taken them out of the storage racks and propped them against the walls of the studio, in the order you told me to. I led both the Goldstone woman and Xavier back there. She took one look at them—"

"Oh, God." Lacey ordered herself to breathe. "What?"

"—and she turned to Xavier and me—we were standing behind her. She waved at us, a shooing gesture, with the back of her hand. 'Leave me alone,' she said. 'Give a woman some space.'"

"So? You and Xavier—"

"We went out to the kitchen area. I bought an espresso machine, did I tell you? We made lattes."

"You and Xavier made lattes, while Belinda Goldstone looked at my paintings."

"That's right. She was in there forever."

"And when she came out?"

"She was very quiet. I offered her a latte. She said she had to get back to the gallery."

"And that's all?"

"You should have seen her face."

"Why? What was wrong with it?"

"Nothing. She loved what she saw."

"You *think* she loved what she saw."

"No. I *know* she loved what she saw. She'll be calling you, just wait."

"Wait?" Lacey let out a wild laugh. "*Wait?* I'll go crazy…"

"Call Xavier. Maybe she said something more to him after they left."

She did call Xavier. He didn't answer, so she left him a message.

He called back two hours later, after she'd nursed Rosie and changed her diaper and spent the rest of the time pacing the floor.

Xavier said virtually the same thing Barnaby had said. That he was sure Belinda Goldstone would be calling her soon.

"Soon? When is *soon?*"

"It's Friday, Lace. And it's after three. The working week is over."

"Oh. Great. That's just great."

"I'm sure she'll call you Monday. Or sometime next week."

"I might have a nervous breakdown before then."

"A nervous breakdown would be counterproductive. My advice is to work."

"Work."

"Yes. And do…whatever mothers do with their infants. Go someplace wonderful for dinner. Make love with your husband. Live your life and live it well."

"If Belinda Goldstone happens to call you—"

"She won't. Not about you. It's between you and her now. I gave her your number."

"She asked for it?"

"Yes. So settle down. Wait. She will call. She'll ask you to meet with her. She'll offer to become your dealer. And she'll want to discuss your first show with her gallery."

"You're talking about it as if it's really going to happen."

"Because it is. Wait and see—and calm down. You deserve this, Lace. Remember that. You've worked long and hard to get to this point."

Lacey decided not to tell Logan about the calls from L.A. She had no real news yet, and he'd seemed so cool on the subject the other time they'd discussed it. She decided it would be wiser to wait until she had something concrete to say.

By the time he came home, after eight, she had settled down considerably. She'd even spent a couple of hours in her studio working on a painting she'd started of the twins.

He brought flowers. And his eyes were tender and hopeful.

He didn't mention Jenna or the argument of the night before. But he did say, "I missed you all day. I couldn't wait to get home and get my arms around you."

He gave her the flowers and then hardly allowed her the time to put them in a vase before he was pulling her close and raining kisses on her upturned face.

"I love kissing you. It's something about the way you smell, like no one else, so damn sweet…" His lips moved down to her throat. He began to draw on the skin.

She laughed, putting up a playful struggle. "Remember. Tomorrow night. The Health Aid Society Banquet."

He growled against her neck and took his bruising kiss lower.

A few minutes later, he was leading her toward the stairs, stopping in the breakfast room and the hall, first to remove her big shirt and then her skinny tube top, which he'd already slid down so it was bunched around her waist.

On the stairs, he helped her out of her shoes. He took away her capri pants in the balcony hall. By the time they reached their bedroom, all she had left was a pair of red bikini panties.

He got rid of them, too.

Then he guided her down onto the bed and he kissed her all over, until she moaned and writhed and forgot all about the love words he never said and the sister he wouldn't visit and his cool, distant responses when she'd hinted at a breakthrough in her career.

* * *

The next night, at the Meadow Valley Country Club, Lacey and Logan shared a table with Dan and Fiona and Helen and her husband, Bud. After the food and the speeches, there was dancing. Lacey whirled in her husband's arms and thought that being the wife of a handsome doctor did have its moments—especially when the doctor in question was Logan.

They danced for a half hour without stopping, waiting on the floor as each number ended, and then picking up the rhythm again when a new song began. Finally, though, the five-piece combo took a break.

Lacey whispered in her husband's ear, "We're going to have to leave soon, I'm afraid."

He knew what she meant. "Are you all right?"

"So far." Her breasts were beginning to feel just a bit uncomfortable. "But I'd say that Rosie's probably getting hungry and I would prefer not to have a leaking accident—and don't look now, but that nice pharmaceutical supplies salesman is headed our way. I think it's time I paid a visit to the ladies' room."

Logan held her closer and murmured for her ears alone, "Great. Leave me when I need you most."

She kissed him on the cheek. "I'll be back. Then we'll go."

The salesman was closing in as Logan reluctantly released her.

Lacey followed the arrows to the club's black and white marble ladies' room, which was, surprisingly enough, unoccupied. She proceeded down to the end stall.

She'd barely shut the door and engaged the latch

when she heard the main door open again. High heels tapped against the marble tiles.

"No one here." That was Helen Sanderson's voice, pitched low, but quite clear. Voices carried easily, amplified against the cool marble walls.

Lacey froze, feeling awkward and a little silly, wondering if she should announce her own presence, then thinking how gauche that would sound. She heard a stall door open, then another, and then two sets of footsteps again, this time entering the stalls.

"She really is lovely," Helen said. Two latches clicked shut. "And quite charming, as well."

"Yes." That was Fiona. "Those gorgeous big blue eyes and that angelic face—you did hear the story, didn't you?"

Dread. Lacey felt it. Like a lead weight in her stomach. She knew what was coming.

And it was.

"Of course," Helen said. "Jenna Bravo's sister. An affair that resulted in pregnancy. A marriage was probably the best choice, under the circumstances. And they certainly do appear devoted to each other."

Lacey leaned her forehead against the cool metal of the stall door thinking, *It's too late to speak up now.*

She lifted her head, straightened her shoulders. Buck up, she silently instructed herself. The things they're saying are only the truth.

"Yes," said Fiona. "I think it's all working out rather well. It's obvious Logan is thoroughly taken with her. I think a lot of it is—oh, how to say it—physical? But there's nothing necessarily wrong with that, now is there? Over time, I'm sure the relationship will deepen and mature."

One toilet flushed, and then the other.

Lacey thought, *That's all. They're going to shut up now.*

They weren't.

Helen said, "I understand you've been taking her under your wing."

"I have," Fiona replied. "I really do enjoy her. And I think, as time goes by, she'll settle down. She did have a few problems as a high school girl. Wild antics and crazy pranks. And she ran away a lot, from what I've been able to find out. But all that's in the past. Nothing to worry about now, from what I can see. I'm trying to guide her along a little, to get her involved with the auxiliary at Miner's General and a few other important pet projects of mine. She insists she doesn't have the time, that she's going to *make* something of herself as an artist."

"So I heard." The stall latches clicked again, the women's shoes echoed on the marble tiles.

Lacey remained absolutely still. She thought, *I will be quiet. I will be tactful. I will do what my sister would have done under these circumstances. I will wait here with my mouth shut until they leave.*

Water ran in the basins. Fiona declared, "Marrying Logan is the best thing that ever could have happened to her. She's been living hand-to-mouth in Los Angeles the past several years, hoping her *art* would someday support her." The water stopped. Lacey heard the whisk-thump of paper towels being pulled from dispensers. "It's sad, I think, a bright, sweet girl like that, with such big dreams and no hope of their ever coming true."

That did it. It was just one condescending remark too many.

Lacey whirled and hit the flush button, though she'd never gotten around to using the toilet. Maybe it was small-minded of her, but she found the corresponding hush from the sink area gratifying in the extreme.

Then she turned back to the door, clicked open the latch and exited the stall, shoulders back and chin aimed high.

Fiona and Helen turned from the mirrors with matching expressions of mortified horror.

Fiona found her voice first. It sounded slightly choked. "Uh. Lacey. Oh, my…"

Lacey granted Fiona a blinding smile as she stepped up to the sink and flipped on the goldtone faucet. She squirted soap onto her palm and stuck her hands beneath the water, sending a second smile, as dazzling as the first, in the doctor's direction.

She said sweetly, "You two really ought to find a more private setting for your intimate conversations."

Fiona started to speak, and then coughed instead. Helen merely continued to look dismayed.

Lacey turned off the water and yanked a towel from the dispenser. "I'll tell you what. Sometime in the next year or so, I'm having a major show of some of my most recent paintings, in Los Angeles—have you heard about my show?"

Both women, in unison, swung their heads from side-to-side.

Lacey wadded her towel and tossed it in the trash.

"Well, you have now. And of course, you will both be invited. Can I count on you to come?"

"Ahem, well..." said Helen.

"I...really...I..." stammered Fiona.

"A simple yes or no from each of you will do."

Fiona blinked. And then she actually said, "Of course I'll come, Lacey."

And Helen said, "Well. Thank you for inviting me. I'll do my best to attend."

"Terrific." Lacey fluffed her hair and straightened her midnight-blue sequined sheath—no leaks yet, thank God. "I can't tell you how much I'll enjoy having both of you there." She turned, edged around the dazed-looking Fiona and headed for the exit door, pausing before she went out to remark pleasantly, "This has been a great party. But the chicken Kiev was just a tad dry, didn't you think?"

Fiona and Helen looked at each other. They both nodded.

"Yes," said Fiona.

"A little dry," Helen concurred.

Chapter 15

During the drive home, Lacey told Logan all about the incident in the ladies' room.

He did not look pleased when she related the things Fiona and Helen had said, but then a half-smile curved his lips as she described how she'd marched out of the stall and spoken right up to them.

And then he said what she already knew. "You probably would have been wiser to have spoken up right away—or to have left it alone and kept quiet until they left."

"I agree, but you know how I am." She leaned across the console and touched a finger to his lips. "And I saw that smile. You don't completely disapprove of the way I reacted."

He caught her hand, kissed the fingers, then let go to execute a turn.

"And besides," she said. "I *like* Fiona. And Helen's basically okay, too. They can be a little stuffy, but they're still good at heart—a lot like you, actually, in that respect."

"Oh, I'm stuffy, am I?"

"If the lab coat fits…but it's okay. I love you anyway. And if I hadn't stood up to those women right then, I would have had to do it later, or ended up resenting them. This way, we all know where we stand."

"No doubt about that." He cast her a look. "And what about this L.A. opening you invented out of thin air?"

She hesitated, not sure she wanted to get into the subject of the call she hoped to receive from Belinda Goldstone.

He prompted, "Well?"

"I think I'll play that by ear."

He sent her another glance, an amused one this time. "I guess you will."

She waited a little nervously for him to say something else about the supposed art show. But he didn't. So she let it go. She'd stick with her original plan and tell him after she knew more—if it turned out there actually *was* more. It was always possible that both Barnaby and Xavier had misread the art dealer's reaction.

Maybe, in the end, there would be no call from Belinda Goldstone. That thought made her feel more than a little deflated.

But then she reminded herself of the painting she'd been working on, the one of the twins. It was coming together pretty well. She *was* working again. She *did* have talent and she wasn't going to give up, whether Belinda Goldstone offered to be her dealer or not.

* * *

Rosie was hungry when they got home. And Lacey was more than ready to feed her. Logan paid the sitter and drove her home.

When he returned, they took Rosie to bed with them. They snuggled in, all three of them, and turned on the television in the sitting area to a channel that was playing an old Hitchcock thriller. Rosie fell asleep first, cuddled between them.

Lacey dropped off soon after that. She woke a little later to find her husband snoring softly and her baby still sound asleep as well, sucking her tiny fist. On the television, Tippi Hedren screamed under brutal attack by a flock of furious crows. Lacey found the remote and pointed it at the television.

The screen went black. She kissed her baby and brushed her husband's dark hair off his forehead.

"And Fiona thinks it's mostly physical," she murmured fondly. Then she pulled the covers close and joined her family in sleep.

Fiona called the next day to apologize. "I was completely out of line to speak that way of you. I've just been agonizing that you're going to hate me."

Lacey said, "I don't hate you, Fiona. I like you. And I agree with a lot of what you said last night."

"You…you do?"

"Absolutely. Marrying Logan *is* the best thing that ever happened to me. And since *I'm* the best thing that ever happened to him, I'd say we're an excellent match."

Fiona took a moment to digest that bit of logic. Then she chuckled. "Lacey, my dear, you are a breath of fresh air. Tell me, can I still count on you for Saturday? The Aid to the Indigent rummage sale?"

Lacey assured Fiona that yes, she'd be there to handle a booth.

"And about those reminder calls…"

"I made the first set already. And I'll call everyone again in the next couple of days."

"You are an angel."

"Well, I wouldn't go *that* far."

At one o'clock Monday afternoon, Belinda Goldstone called.

At first, she spoke in hushed, awestruck tones, praising the nine figure studies she'd seen in Barnaby Cole's studio, calling them fresh and exciting and "hauntingly sensual."

Then she got down to business. "As I'm sure you've guessed by now, I would like to represent your work. Now, I know this is a lot to take in all at once, but as it turns out, I have an unexpected hole in my gallery's schedule."

One of her artists, she explained, had moved to New York.

"The SoHo scene has gone to his head," Belinda grumbled. "The wretched little ingrate has jumped ship to go with a dealer there. He was scheduled to show in March. I'd like to put you in his slot. We'd hang the paintings I saw at Barnaby Cole's studio, of course. And do you have anything else that's ready to show… or *could* be ready by then?"

Lacey felt slightly dizzy. Six months. Six months

until her first major show, a *one-woman* show. With Belinda Goldstone's gallery.

"The silence is deafening," said Belinda. "Am I pushing too fast? We could wait until next October. Would that be better? That will give you a full year to—"

"No. No, March should be fine."

"You sound unsure."

"I'm not. It's just…what you said. A lot to take in. But I have a few other paintings stored at Barnaby's. You could take a look at them. And I've been working on some things more recently, too." She was thinking of the painting of Mira and Maud, of some ideas she had that would center on Rosie—and the sketches she'd done of Logan, asleep in the cabin in Wyoming. She'd been planning to do more with those very soon.

"We must meet in person as soon as you can manage it," said Belinda. "You'll see. The next six months will fly by. We have to get started. We have to firm up the business end. And I want to visit your friend Barnaby again—but together this time—to discuss the work you have at his studio. When can you come?"

Lacey heard herself announcing that she could come right away.

Logan didn't get home until after nine that night.

Lacey fed him and listened to the details of a doctor's day: the seven-year-old who had almost died of an asthma attack, the sweet elderly widower who refused to take his meds, the thirty-five-year-old woman who had fallen off her roof trying to coax her cat down out of a maple tree.

"Compound fracture of the left tibia." He shook his head. "What a mess. Shouldn't an adult woman know better?"

Lacey wiggled her eyebrows at him. "You're asking me?"

They laughed together. The previous September, right at the end of their five-day affair, Lacey had put her foot through the ceiling of one of the upstairs bedrooms in the house that had been her mother's. She'd been searching the attic for Jenna's cat, which had vanished not long before. She'd ended up with a broken foot—and the cat had shown up over a week later, in another part of town.

"What is it with women and cats?" Logan asked.

Since the question sounded thoroughly rhetorical, Lacey only shrugged.

Once Logan had eaten, Lacey poured him a brandy and led him upstairs. They sat on the sofa in the sitting area of their bedroom.

He swirled his brandy, sipped and set his glass on the coffee table. "Should we check on Rosie?"

"I'd say we have approximately…" she glanced at her watch, and then at the baby monitor across the room, on the nightstand by the bed "…a half hour, and we'll be hearing from her."

"Better enjoy every second of quiet, then."

"My sentiments exactly."

He laid his arm along the sofa back. She snuggled up close and leaned her head on his shoulder.

His lips brushed the crown of her head. "It's good to be home."

"Um…" She rubbed her cheek against the starched

cloth of his dress shirt, thinking how she liked this time the best, in the evenings, when he came home to her and they sat together—talking, laughing, sharing what had happened in their respective days.

"So tell me," he said, "what's been going on around here?"

It was the moment she'd been waiting for, time to tell him her news.

Her pulse had picked up. She was a little nervous, a little worried about how he would take this, given the way he'd reacted the last time she'd mentioned the dealer who just might be interested in showing her work.

Logan laughed, a low, pleasant sound, warm and deep in her ear. "What? Total boredom? Nothing to report?"

She ordered her silly heartbeat to slow down. "As a matter of fact, I do have some news."

"What?"

She raised her head from its comfortable niche on his shoulder. It seemed wiser, somehow, to look at him when she told him.

He frowned. "What? Is something wrong?"

"No. No, not at all."

"Then…?"

Her mouth had gone as dry as a long stretch of desert road. She gulped, licked her lips.

"Lacey? What's the matter?"

"Nothing. Really. I only…"

"You only what?"

She said it. "Belinda Goldstone called today."

He just looked at her.

She gulped again. "Belinda…offered me a show—my *own* show—at her gallery, six months from now."

"Your own show," he repeated, each word slow and cautious.

She nodded. What was he thinking? She couldn't tell. She barreled ahead. "She needs to meet with me right away. So I said I'd fly down to L.A. tomorrow, and stay at least until Saturday. We'll get to know each other a little, make some decisions about what to include in the show—well, I mean, beyond those nine paintings I told you about, the ones of you?" She made herself pause, aware she was talking way too fast.

A black hole of silence followed. Cold fingers of dread tracked their way down her spine. He wasn't taking this well. He wasn't taking it well at all.

She didn't know what else to do, so she babbled out more information. "And Friday night, as it turns out, there's a show opening at Belinda's gallery. So I said I'd be there for that. It will be a great way to get the word out that she'll be handling my work."

She stopped again, for a breath—and because it seemed that she ought to give him a chance to talk.

He didn't talk. He just went on staring at her. She couldn't bear that. She prattled on. "I'd love for you to go, too, if you could manage it. I booked a flight for me and Rosie today, while I was making all the other arrangements, but I'm sure I could find one for all of us, if you'd come. I'm leaving tomorrow, staying with my friend Adele. But if you come, we can just go ahead and get a—"

He raised a hand. She fell silent in mid-sentence. "Let me get this straight," he said. "You're dragging

Rosie to L.A. with you. And you're leaving tomorrow."
His voice was utterly flat.

She stared at him, shocked by the look of pure disdain in his eyes.

"Well?" he demanded.

She made herself answer in a low, careful tone, all her former manic brightness fled. "Yes, Logan. I'm leaving tomorrow. And as for Rosie, well, what else would I do? She's nursing, so I have to be around to feed her."

"You're dragging her all over L.A. with you, to meet an art dealer? And to some art party?"

"No. I'm not dragging her anywhere. I have it all worked out. Adele loves babies. She's promised to babysit."

"All right. So you're flying to Los Angeles tomorrow to meet Belinda Goldstone. You're taking our daughter with you, and some artist friend of yours has promised to watch her."

"Logan, if you'd only—"

"Just tell me. Have I got it right?"

She pulled back to her side of the sofa, shock giving way to anger—anger that tightened her stomach and brought a hot flush to her cheeks. "Yes," she said, her tone as flat as his. "You've got it right."

"I suppose you knew about this the other night," he accused, "when you came up with that crack about your L.A. opening to put Helen and Fiona in their places. You knew then, didn't you, and you never said a word to me?"

The anger inside her burned hotter. She kept her voice low with great effort. "No, Logan. I didn't know.

I *hoped.* But I didn't know any of this until Belinda called this afternoon."

That stopped him. For a few seconds, anyway. But he wasn't about to let the fact that he'd judged her unfairly slow him down for long. He shook his head—in disgust, or disbelief, or some distressing combination of the two. "You could have talked to me before you made your plans."

Stay cool, she told herself. *It's not going to help if you start yelling at him.*

"I know," she said, each word precise, strictly controlled. "I probably should have talked to you first. But I got excited. I agreed to meet her right away. And then I didn't want to call you and try to discuss it while you were taking care of patients. It just seemed wiser to go ahead and make my plans, and then explain everything when you got home."

He made a low sound in his throat, a sound that dismissed her, a sound that disregarded everything she'd said. "This is totally irresponsible of you. Rosie is barely two months old. And you are nursing. You can't leave her for long."

Lacey kept her mouth shut. Rosie often went as long as four hours between feedings. And there *was* such a thing as a breast pump, after all. But she knew her husband wouldn't hear her if she told him those things. No point in wasting her breath.

He sneered, "I've never met this—what did you say her name was?"

She sighed. "Adele Levenson."

"How do I know that this Adele Levenson is someone reliable?"

That really grated. She couldn't keep quiet, couldn't hold back the sarcasm. "Well, I don't know, Logan. How about because I say so and I'm your wife—and you *trust* me?"

He looked away, picked up his brandy glass, gulped down a too-big sip. She sat, waiting, watching him regroup, knowing just how his mind worked.

He'd come on way too strong, and he was realizing that now, remembering what he was. A *reasonable* man.

"Listen," he said at last, gently now. "You've got to look at this logically. It's just not a good time for something like this. You have a two-month-old baby. And responsibilities here. I thought you told me that on Saturday, you were helping Fiona out at one of her charity events."

She had to suppress a groan of disbelief. "Oh, Logan. Do you *hear* yourself? You're saying I should turn down the most important career opportunity that's ever come my way because I promised Fiona I'd help out at a rummage sale."

Now he looked wounded. "The rummage sale is something that you agreed to do."

"Yes, I did. But I'll call Fiona first thing tomorrow. I'm sure she'll understand. Everything—all of this—can be worked out. As I said, I have friends in L.A. who will help me with Rosie. And we have Mrs. Hopper. She's a jewel and you know she'll take good care of you while we're away, unless—" she tried one more time "—you decide to come with me?"

"I can't get away now. It's impossible."

"All right, then you'll stay home. But as I just said,

we can work it out. It'll be a challenge, yes. But not an insurmountable one."

He had that intractable look on his face, an expression she'd always disliked—and never more so than now. "It's not good for Rosie," he said again. "You can't just run off and leave her with your flighty artistic friends."

She held on to her patience—by a thread. "Logan. Just because a person is an artist doesn't necessarily mean they're flighty. Or irresponsible."

"I don't know these friends of yours."

She closed her eyes, dragged in a breath. "We're going in circles."

"I don't want you to do this."

"I got that. Loud and clear. And my question is, *why?*"

"I've told you. For a number of reasons."

"Yes, you have. A number of trumped-up, fake, completely meaningless reasons."

"Meaningless? I'd hardly call it meaningless that I want my wife at home with me, and I want to know that my daughter is being well cared-for."

"Oh, come on. I'll be gone for five days. And Rosie, as I've said about ten times now, will be fine."

"It's not a good idea."

Oh, how she longed to start shouting. But somehow she managed to hold her anger and frustration in check. She leaned closer to him. "Why won't you tell me what's really going on here? Please. I want to understand."

He sat back, reached for his brandy again. "I've told you my concerns. They're completely reasonable."

"Reasonable," she repeated.

"Yes," he said, "reasonable."

"You know, it wouldn't be hard at all for me to learn to hate that word."

He emptied the glass and then set it down a little too hard. "I don't want to discuss it further. Call that dealer and tell her you're not coming."

Her mouth dropped open. "What did you say?"

"You heard me."

"Tell me this isn't happening. Tell me this is some nightmare I've stumbled into, that in a moment or two, I'm going to wake up."

"Just call that damn dealer."

"No."

He glowered at her.

She wanted to fling herself at him and pound on his chest. She wanted to scream rude, *un*reasonable invectives, to rant and rail at his impossible, pigheaded, unbearable male arrogance.

But she didn't. She held her temper and she spoke with low and hard-won control. She said, "I love you, Logan. We have a good life together. Yesterday, I told Fiona that you were the best thing that ever happened to me. And I meant it. You came to me in Wyoming when I didn't even know how much I needed you, and you refused to go away. You stayed at my side to see our daughter safely born. You convinced me to marry you. And I have been grateful, so grateful, that you did. Because on the whole, we're good together. I have been happy being your wife.

"You've never said that *you* love *me*. But I've learned to accept that. I've told myself that you love me by your actions, and that someday, when you're ready, you'll come to me and say your love in words."

He started to speak.

"No," she said, "wait. I'm not finished. I have gone into your world and learned to enjoy it—the upscale business parties, the charity dinners, the good works everyone seems to expect from a doctor's wife. I've made, or am making, space for all that in my life. For your sake. And I would like very much for you to return the favor. So far, you haven't."

"I—"

"No," she said. "Wait."

His eyes spoke volumes—angry, hard, ugly volumes—but he kept his mouth shut.

She said, "I've asked you to come with me to hear my friends play their music. You've put me off. Okay, I told myself, he'll come eventually. Just be patient. Give it time. I've wanted you to come with me to visit my sister. You put me off again. I've said to myself, All right, he loved her and she hurt him and I'll give him some time on that, too."

Lacey stood. "But this, I can't give you time on. People only get so many great chances in life. For me, this is one. It really won't wait. And there's no reason, other than your completely *un*reasonable possessiveness, that it needs to wait. I am not going to turn Belinda Goldstone down. Rosie and I are leaving tomorrow. We'll be back Saturday afternoon. And that is all there is to that."

Chapter 16

Logan recognized the look on his wife's face.

On this issue, there would be no compromise.

She was going to Los Angeles tomorrow and nothing he could say would change her mind.

He'd told her all of the reasons she *shouldn't* go, and she refused to hear them.

Rosie chose that moment to let out a cry.

Logan glanced toward the baby monitor, then back into his wife's flushed, furious face. Lacey stayed where she was for a grim few seconds, staring down at him with fire in her eyes. He stared right back at her, his will meeting hers. Rosie let out another wail.

Lacey spun on her heel and left him there.

His beeper went off about two minutes later. He removed the device from his belt and checked the number: his exchange.

Five minutes after that, he stopped at the threshold of Rosie's room where Lacey sat in the rocker, nursing their child. She hadn't turned on the light. A wedge of brightness from the hall fixture behind him spilled across the floor, not quite reaching the chair where she and the baby rocked.

"Emergency," he said. Ordinarily, he would have given her some explanation. He would have said, That asthma patient's had another severe attack.

But not tonight. Tonight he didn't want to explain anything to her.

"I don't know when I'll be back."

She looked at him. Her eyes were somber and far away. In the dim light, they seemed strangely without color. "All right," she said. "I won't wait up."

He turned and left her in the dark.

In the morning, over an otherwise silent breakfast, she told him that her flight left from Sacramento at four that afternoon. "I'll just take my SUV and use the long-term parking."

"No. I'll take you."

She would have smiled at him in pleasure at the gesture, if only he hadn't been looking at her through eyes as cold as a midwinter night. "Thanks, but it isn't necessary, honestly. I can just—"

"I said, I'll drive you. Is there some reason you'd prefer I didn't?"

"Of course not. I just thought that it might be hard for you to manage the time away from the office on such short notice."

"If I couldn't manage it, I wouldn't have offered."

"All right, Logan. Thank you. I'll ride with you."

"When is your flight back?"

"I should arrive in Sacramento at four-thirty Saturday afternoon. I'll leave you the flight number and Adele's number and Barnaby's, too."

"Fine."

He didn't speak again until it was time for him to leave for the office, when he said, "I'll be here to pick you up at two."

"I'll be ready."

He left without granting her his usual fond goodbye peck.

She had plenty to do that morning. She got her portfolio in order, tucking in some sketches that would help her to explain her works in progress to Belinda. She wrote out detailed instructions for Mrs. Hopper, packed for herself and Rosie and then called Fiona.

Fiona wished her well, and made her promise that she'd help out with something called Food for Friends. "We have our big food drive next month, for Thanksgiving."

"Count me in."

"I knew I could. Good luck in L.A."

"Thanks. It's a big step."

"And your paintings will be hanging in a gallery in March?"

"That's right."

"Remember, you're getting Dan and me tickets to the opening."

Lacey promised she wouldn't forget.

She called the twins next, first Mira, then Maud.

Mira let out a shout of glee when she heard the news.

"Call the minute you get back," she instructed. "Maud and I will want to know everything."

Maud's reaction was a mirror to her twin's. Their unbridled enthusiasm helped to cheer Lacey up—as the disagreement with Logan dragged her down. She tried to put images of his scowling face from her mind as she hurried to get ready.

The ride to the airport was as silent as breakfast had been. Rosie fussed some and Logan demanded suspiciously, "Is she feverish?"

Lacey reached over the seat to press her palm to Rosie's brow. "Feels normal to me."

Her husband shot her a glance in which skepticism vied for dominance with brooding hostility. She bit her lip to keep herself from saying something she'd later regret.

At the terminal, Logan helped her check her luggage, then carried Rosie's car seat, diaper bag and Lacey's bulky portfolio to the boarding area for her.

She and Rosie boarded early. Logan helped with that, getting the steward to find a place for the portfolio and strapping Rosie's car carrier in the seat next to Lacey's.

Then he muttered a gruff, "Goodbye," and turned to go.

Rosie rested on Lacey's shoulder, cradled on her left arm. She reached out with her right and caught his elbow. "Logan?"

He faced her again, unsmiling.

She pulled him to her and kissed him, a quick, hard kiss, on the mouth. "See you Saturday."

"Yes." His eyes were distant, his voice without inflection. "I'll be here." Rosie made a cooing sound. He laid his hand on her small back. "Bye, Rosie." Those words, at least, had feeling in them.

Lacey watched him walk up the narrow aisle away from her, until he disappeared through the exit. Then she strapped Rosie into her seat.

Adele met Lacey and Rosie at LAX and drove them straight to her shingled bungalow-style house in Pasadena. The two women spent the early evening playing catch-up, filling each other in on their separate lives in the months since Lacey had left L.A.

Adele Levenson was in her mid-fifties, with a cap of wild gray curls and a body of Rubenesque proportions. She wore flowing dresses in dramatic colors: hot turquoise, emerald green, yellow as bright as lemons in sunlight. She'd been married and divorced and had three grown children living in different parts of the state. She confessed that she'd enjoyed her marriage— at least the first ten years of it. And she'd loved raising her children.

"But I love this, too." She gestured with a wide sweep of both arms. "My own house. Time just for me. The luxury of working whenever the mood strikes."

They spent a couple of hours on the sunporch in back, which Adele used as her studio. Lacey admired the new landscapes Adele showed her, struck as always by the way Adele's watercolors shimmered with vivid color and gorgeous washes of golden light.

"You just get better and better," Lacey told her friend.

Around nine, after Adele had served a dinner of lamb chops and wild rice and Lacey had put Rosie down to sleep in the spare room, the two women went out onto the big stone front porch. They sat on the porch swing in the moonlight and listened to the sounds of night birds and the whispering whoosh of cars going by down the drive.

"You seem…a little sad," Adele said. "A little pensive. It's in your eyes. And in your voice. Is it something you'd like to talk about?"

Lacey shook her head.

"I'm here to listen, if you need me."

Lacey reached out, put her hand on Adele's bright sleeve. "Thanks. I'll remember that."

At a little after ten, Lacey excused herself. She went to the bedroom she shared with her daughter, took out her cell phone and dialed the house on Orchard Street. After four rings, the answering machine picked up. Lacey listened to her own voice instructing her to leave a message.

Then she said, "Logan, it's me. I just…wanted you to know we got in all right. We're at Adele's now, all settled in for the night. I…I love you. Don't ever forget that."

She hung up feeling foolish, wondering if he'd had to work late, or if he'd rushed out to the hospital to handle some emergency. Or if maybe he'd been standing right there as she left her message, listening to each word that she said, unwilling to pick up the phone and talk to her.

The next day, Adele insisted that Lacey use her car. "It's ridiculous for you to rent one. I never go out that much anyway. We can share while you're here."

So Lacey drove Adele's comfortable old Chrysler into downtown L.A., where she met with Belinda at Barnaby's place. Belinda liked the seven other paintings Lacey showed her. And she seemed honestly enthusiastic when Lacey described her ideas for the three or four more pieces she thought she could finish before the show in March.

"Come see me at the gallery, tomorrow," Belinda said.

Lacey agreed to be there at eleven. Then she gave Barnaby a big hug and promised she'd find some way to get together with him before she left for home. She raced back to Adele's, her breasts aching and full, to feed Rosie her lunch.

That evening, after she'd told Adele good-night, she called Logan again. And got no answer. She left another message, a brief one. "It's me. Everything's going fine. I love you. I'll see you Saturday."

Strange, she thought when she hung up. Last winter, it was Logan calling me, leaving messages I never answered.

And just look at us now—the situation reversed.

She'd thought they'd come so far, in the two months of their marriage. But now she wondered if they'd made any progress at all.

She loved him.

She would always love him.

But she was beginning to ask herself the scariest kind of question: Would they get through this with their marriage intact? Could she, perhaps, have been right from the first about the two of them, that they were two people distinctly *not* meant for each other?

The way it looked now, either she gave up her dreams for him, or she would lose him. What kind of choice was that?

And why would a basically good man—and she did believe that Logan *was* a good man—force her to make such a choice?

Logan got in after midnight.

The house seemed too empty, too damn gray and dreary, without Lacey there. He'd stayed away as long as he could, eating dinner out, then heading back to the hospital to check on a couple of patients in critical care.

After the hospital, he'd made a last stop at the office. There was always a stack of stuff on his desk crying out to be dealt with. He spent a couple of hours plowing through the pile.

And then, because he couldn't think of any more ways to avoid it, he returned to the house on Orchard Street. He went straight to the answering machine on the counter in the kitchen. The message light blinked at him.

He pushed the button—and he heard her voice.

He played the message three times, longing coursing through him like a pulse.

I love you, she said, just as she had the night before. Only then, she had added, *Don't ever forget that.*

I love you….

Don't ever forget that….

The words echoed through his brain, along with all the things he kept trying not to think about, those hard things she had said to him the night before she left.

This really can't wait. And there's no reason, other

than your completely unreasonable possessiveness, that it needs to wait.

I have gone into your world and learned to enjoy it. I would like very much for you to return the favor. So far, you haven't.

I've asked you to come with me to hear my friends play... To visit my sister... You've never said that you love me...

Logan leaned on the counter and pressed his head between his hands. "Stop, damn it!" he shouted at the silent, empty room.

It worked, more or less. It silenced the remembered echo of her voice.

But it didn't make what she'd said any less true.

Thursday evening, Adele invited Xavier and Barnaby and Xavier's wife, Sophia, to dinner. Barnaby had a previous commitment he couldn't get out of, but Xavier and Sophia came. It was a good evening, full of laughter and interesting talk. Xavier held Rosie, declared her a beauty and said she smelled like peaches. He and his wife left at a little after ten. He had an early flight to New York the next day.

At ten-thirty, after she'd bid Adele good-night, Lacey called her husband for the third time. He didn't answer. She left a three-sentence message that ended with *I love you.*

Then she got into bed with her daughter and tried to sleep.

It was no good.

At ten-forty-five, she called home again.

After three rings, her husband surprised her. He answered.

"Hello." The way he said that single word made her heart ache. He sounded so lonely, so very far away.

And something in that hollow, distant voice reminded her poignantly of his father. Lacey hadn't known Logan Sr. particularly well. She remembered that he had dark eyes, like Logan's, and that he rarely smiled. He'd been a very serious man, a man who set high standards and expected his only son to live up to them.

And live up to them Logan did. Perhaps too well in some ways.

"Hello," Logan said again, an impatient edge creeping in.

"Hello, Logan. It's me."

He hesitated, then said her name, "Lacey…"

Now, that's more like it, she thought. That sounded almost tender.

But then again, maybe she was just a victim of a bad case of wishful thinking. "Did you get my messages?"

He took a moment to answer, as if he suspected she meant to trick him with such a question. Then he said, "I got them. Last night and the night before."

"You didn't call back," she said, thinking: Brilliant. State the painfully obvious.

He cleared his throat. "You didn't say anything about wanting me to call you back."

Ohmigoodness, were they a pair or what? She sighed. "Next time I'll make my desires clearer—I also called about fifteen minutes ago."

"I just walked in the door."

"I see. Well, then. I guess you didn't get that one."

"Right. I didn't. How's Rosie?"

"She's doing great. She's asleep now, otherwise I'd let you talk to her."

A silence, then he chuckled. To Lacey's ears, the sound was like soothing balm spread gently on a throbbing wound.

He asked with reluctant humor, "Learned to talk in two days, has she?"

Tears misted her vision. She blinked them away. "Children can really surprise you. Especially the bright ones."

"Lacey..."

She clutched the phone tighter. "Yes? What?"

"Uh—how's it going there?"

"Um—good. Really good. I met Belinda. I have a positive feeling about her. She's exciting, but soothing at the same time. If that makes any sense."

"You'll have to explain it to me in more depth... when you get home."

Home. That sounded lovely. "Yes. Yes, I'll do that. She, Belinda, I mean, she liked the other things I showed her. Some older paintings I had at Barnaby's. And she seemed excited about my sketches. Of course, we both agreed you never can tell. You can have the most wonderful ideas, but then, in the execution, everything falls apart. Or it all changes, and it's not what you thought it would be when you started...which isn't necessarily bad. It might be *better* than what you conceived in the planning stages. It might—" She realized she was babbling and cut herself off. "Anyway, we'll just have to wait and see what else I come up with. And

Belinda's open to that, which is another thing I like about her."

"So you're saying, it's all working out."

"Yes. That's exactly what I'm saying."

He was silent. And so was she. For a moment, they just listened to each other breathe.

Finally, he asked softly, "Lace?"

Hope. She could feel it growing inside her, effervescent as the bubbles in a glass of champagne, warm as sunlight streaming in an open window. "Yes?"

"I..."

"What, Logan?"

"I want you to know..." The sentence wandered off unfinished.

She clutched the phone and waited.

At last, he said, "Look. We'll talk. About a lot of things. When you get home."

She sighed. She had wanted more. A heartfelt apology for the way he'd behaved. An impassioned declaration of undying love. A vow never, ever again to doubt her devotion.

But *we'll talk* wasn't that bad. In fact, *we'll talk* sounded pretty darn good.

"All right," she said. "We'll talk. When I get home."

"And good luck at that big opening tomorrow night."

She laughed. "Thanks, but it's not anything terribly challenging. I'm just putting in an appearance, and then going right back to Adele's in time for Rosie's midnight snack."

"Whatever. Good luck."

"Thank you." She couldn't resist offering one more time. "You could come. You could fly down tomorrow.

I'll pick you up at the airport. You can meet Adele. And I'll take you to Barnaby's loft, show you those incredible nude studies of you that everyone's talking about. And then tomorrow night—"

"No," he said, but in a tender tone. "Let's let it go this time."

This time. That sounded pretty good, too. As if there'd be a next time, when he *would* come with her.

"Logan. I love you."

"Good night, Lace."

"Good night."

"The sun has come out in your eyes," Adele said the next morning. "Something good happened, right? You're feeling better about things."

Lacey sipped her orange juice—the thick, pulpy kind. She'd just squeezed it herself. "Umm. I love orange juice. I love oranges. Doesn't the word seem to just *go* with the fruit? Remember those still lifes you did a few years ago? Oranges in a wooden bowl? I loved those. They were so…orange." She sipped again.

"So," Adele said, "I'm right. You're feeling better."

"Let's say I've discovered there's hope."

"All right. Let's say that."

"Also, I'm leaving tomorrow and I've hardly had a moment with Barnaby."

"So do lunch."

"I should go downtown, to his studio again. I want to see what he's been working on."

"More of that cogs in a machine stuff, from what I understand."

Barnaby painted occasionally, in oil and acrylic. But

his real talent was in sculpture. He worked in metal with a blowtorch. His twisted, tortured metal forms had garnered him more than a little recognition on the national art scene.

Adele got up and poured herself more coffee. "Call him. I'll watch your little rosebud for you."

"Adele, I adore you."

"Good. I'll try to be worthy of such passionate affection."

Lacey found a parking space about ten feet down from the front door of Barnaby's building.

"My lucky day," she said to herself, as she anchored her purse securely onto her shoulder and fed a few coins into the meter.

The buildings around her were big, square industrial structures of chipped concrete and dirty glass. The sidewalk under her feet had cracked and buckled, with time, and from the effects of more than one earthquake, she had no doubt. Trash lined the gutters and piled up in the doorways. The few lost souls on the street looked dirty and desperate and in need of a good meal. There wasn't a tree in sight.

But it all looked beautiful to Lacey.

Because things were going to work out with Logan, she could feel it.

She had it all.

A man she loved heart and soul, a beautiful baby, several dear friends, a talent for doing work she loved— and the distinct possibility that someone would pay for that work in the near future.

And on top of all that, the sun was out, but then, this was L.A., where the sun was *always* out.

She felt like singing, so she did, a few bars from a great old Otis Redding song, "I've Been Loving You Too Long."

She sounded awful. Like a cornered cat, Mira always said.

She laughed, tipping her head back, feeling the sun's benign kiss on her upturned face. "Never was much of a singer…"

Someone had left the street door to Barnaby's building open a crack. She shook her head at it. The neighborhood was a dangerous one. It wasn't wise to leave the doors unlatched for any L.A. desperado to wander in. However, there was a bright side. It saved her the trouble of ringing the bell and waiting for Barnaby to buzz her up.

She pulled open the heavy door and stepped into the shadowy vestibule.

She never saw what hit her. One minute she was turning to make sure the door was firmly shut behind her—and the next the world went black.

Chapter 17

At one-fifteen in the afternoon, Cathy the receptionist stuck her head into the examining room where Logan was going over a medical history.

"You've got a call," Cathy said. "Someone named Adele Levenson on line three. She said it's about—"

He didn't need to hear more. It had to be about Lacey or Rosie. "Thank you, Cathy. I'll be right there." He spoke quite calmly. But his heart had gone into overdrive. It felt damn near tachycardic, beating with a rhythm ragged and way too swift.

Slow down, he thought. *It's probably nothing serious. Some minor problem. Nothing that bad...*

His patient smiled at him when he excused himself. He slipped out the door and went to his private office, where he dropped into his desk chair, grabbed the phone and punched the button that blinked red.

"Hello. This is Logan Severance."

A woman with a gentle voice spoke to him. She said things that couldn't possibly be true.

Lacey had been mugged. Some street punk had attacked her. Her friend Barnaby had found her and called an ambulance.

He heard himself ask, "Head injury, you said?"

"Yes. She was hit on the back of the head. From what I understand, someone knocked her out, grabbed her purse and ran."

"Is she conscious now?"

"No—I don't know. I talked to Barnaby just before I called you. As of then, she hadn't come to."

His heart pounded. His mind swam. He thought, "My God. Rosie..." and realized he'd spoken aloud when Adele Levenson answered him.

"It's all right. Rosie's here with me. You don't have to worry about your little girl."

"What hospital? Where is my wife?"

Adele told him.

He grabbed a pen and wrote it down. "I have your phone number, but I don't know where you live."

She gave him the address.

He scribbled that down, too. "Will you be there, at this number?"

"For a while. I think that's best, with the baby. Lacey borrowed my car, anyway, so I'll have a little trouble trying to go anywhere. But in a few hours, if there's no news, I might try to get a ride to the hospital."

"Do you have a cell phone?"

She said she did. They exchanged numbers. Then he

said, "I'll book the earliest flight I can get. And I'll call you back as soon as I know when I'm coming in."

It took six hours, from the moment Logan hung up the phone until he was striding into ICU at Twin Palms Hospital in Los Angeles.

A neurologist spoke with him. Logan listened, feeling damn near disembodied, one part of his mind screaming, *This is Lacey*—Lacey *we're talking about,* as the information came at him.

She was in a coma.

Lacey. In a *coma*...

The word kept repeating itself in his head. Coma, coma, coma, until it sounded like nonsense syllables, nothing real, nothing that could happen to Lacey, with her bright, inquisitive mind and her naughty sense of humor. Not to Lace, with her musical laughter and her sweet wildness in bed.

"Signs are good, Dr. Severance," the neurologist said.

"Good?" Logan repeated. It was another nonsense syllable.

Good, good, good, good...

"Yes. Very good. Your wife is breathing on her own. We intubated and had her on a respirator for a few hours, then tested and found the respirator unnecessary. EEG and CT scans have revealed nothing out of the ordinary. Of course, we've set up arterial and CVP lines to measure blood pressure and oxygen levels.

"So far, we have minimal cerebral swelling, and we've seen no necessity for invasive procedures. We're going to be monitoring her closely for the slightest change. As I'm sure you're aware, she could wake any minute."

Logan knew the rest of it, the part they never said if they could help it.

Yes, she could wake any minute.

But she might *never* wake.

With head injuries resulting in coma, you waited.

"Can I see her?"

"Of course. Come this way."

He did what the husbands of very ill wives do.

He sat by her bed and he held her hand. He watched hungrily for each slightest movement—the twitching of an eyelid, the tiniest flutter of a muscle in her smooth, white neck.

He spoke with Barnaby Cole—and Adele, who had finally found a ride to the hospital and brought his daughter along. He held Rosie and he fed her milk pumped from the breasts of his unconscious wife.

And he hated himself.

At ten that night, Detective Carla Cruz from the LAPD called him out to the hall. She told him that they'd caught the man who'd attacked his wife. A junkie with a habit to feed. They'd also recovered Lacey's purse, which they were keeping, temporarily anyway, as evidence.

"Whatever cash she might have had is gone, along with any credit cards," Detective Cruz told him regretfully. "But the wallet is still there, as well as her driver's license, some pictures and various store membership cards. And then there are lipsticks and a compact, a small address book—"

"Jenna," Logan said, the name popping into his head and coming right out his mouth.

"Excuse me?"

"I…you said you found an address book in her purse. I was just thinking of someone I should call."

"I'm sorry. That book will be locked up in Evidence now. You can't get to it."

He thanked the detective. She advised him to call the credit card companies and cancel Lacey's cards. And she also said she'd be back in the next twenty-four hours to check on the witness.

Logan understood. They'd want to interview Lacey, if and when she emerged from her unconscious state.

Somehow, that thought soothed him. To imagine cool, efficient-looking Detective Cruz coming back, interviewing Lacey—who would be sitting up in bed by then, blue eyes alert, full lips softly smiling.

As soon as the detective left him, he pulled out his cell phone. He had Mrs. Hopper's number stored there. He dialed the Meadow Valley area code and then punched the proper auto-dial button.

When the housekeeper answered, he told her what had happened and listened to her expressions of shock and concern. Then he asked her to go to the house and get Jenna's phone number from the kitchen drawer address book.

She called him back twenty minutes later.

He thanked her, disconnected the call, and punched up the Key West number the housekeeper had given him.

* * *

Jenna and Mack and their ten-day-old baby, Ian, arrived at Twin Palms Hospital eleven hours later. They'd chartered a jet. Money—and Mack McGarrity had plenty of it—had its uses.

Jenna came into Lacey's room alone, leaving her husband and their baby in the lounge down the hall. Logan was sitting with Lacey, holding her hand, talking to her softly, telling her that she was doing well, that she would get better, that her baby was fine....

He glanced up and Jenna was standing there, her straight blond hair smooth as always around her oval face and her eyes—blue, but a softer, less vivid blue than Lacey's—filled with tears.

He felt relief, that she had come. And affection—the kind of warm feeling one bears a sister. Or a dear friend.

As for the hurt, the bitterness of her leaving him—he could hardly remember it.

The bitterness had been gone for a long time now. Months, really.

Maybe since that September night when Lacey knocked on his door, chocolate cake in hand, determined to console him—and ending up doing so much more.

Changing his life, opening his heart, turning his gray world to full color.

Jenna came to stand beside him. She looked down at her sister. "Oh," she said. "Oh, Lace…"

Carefully, mindful of the lines taped to the back of it, Logan let go of Lacey's hand. He laid it with infinite gentleness on top of the blanket.

He stood.

Jenna turned to him. She held out her arms.

He went into them, seeking solace, seeking reassurance—desperately needing the touch of someone who could understand.

Something inside of him broke wide open. He felt terror and relief, combined.

He couldn't hold back. In a ragged whisper, he breathed his confession against Jenna's shining hair.

"I…never told her. Never said, I love you, Lace. I… held it away from her. I feared the power it would give her, to know how I felt. I let her wonder…if I still loved *you*."

"Logan—"

"No. Please. That's not all. I tried to take her painting away from her. I…I tried to keep her just to myself. She wanted me here, with her, when she came to L.A. She asked me to come any number of times. I should have been with her, when that bastard attacked her. But I wouldn't come. And now, if I've lost her. If I've—"

"Shh," Jenna pulled him closer. "Listen. Listen to me…."

He took her by the arms, looked into her eyes. "Did you hear me? Did you hear what I said?"

She nodded. "I heard. And if you've tried to keep her from her painting, well, shame on you. But about the other. Logan, I think she knows that you love her."

"No. I wouldn't let her know. Wouldn't let her be certain. Even the last time we talked, when I knew how wrong I'd been about so many things, I still couldn't get the damn words out of my mouth. I held back. I said, 'we'll talk, when you get home.' The last thing she said to me was 'I love you.' And all I said in return was 'Good night, Lace.'"

"Logan, she did know."

"No, I—"

"Logan, I told her."

That made no sense. "You…?"

"Yes. I told her. When you were both still in Wyoming. She called and asked my advice about marrying you and I said, 'Do it. He loves you. He's always loved you. He just doesn't know it yet.'"

He gripped her arms harder, his fingers digging in. "Don't tell me good-hearted lies. I need the truth now."

Jenna neither flinched nor wavered. "I'm giving you the truth. My sister knows what love is. And she knows that you love her."

He let go of Jenna's arms and sucked in a breath through a chest that felt as if bands of steel constricted it. "That's something, at least." He turned to Lacey again, took her limp hand. "Do you know?" he asked in a broken voice. "God, let that at least be so. It won't make what I did any more acceptable. But it's better than nothing." He reached up, smoothed the translucent skin of her pale brow.

Jenna took the chair on the other side of the bed. They settled in. To wait some more.

Two hours later, Lacey opened her eyes.

Logan whispered her name.

She turned her head, seeking—and finding him. "Lo-gan," she said, her voice ragged, dry, very low, each syllable an effort—and a triumph. "Logan." And she smiled.

Chapter 18

The next day, they moved her out of ICU.

She got a nice, private room in a medical/surgery wing. After a battery of tests and a lot of poking and prodding by an astonishingly large number of nurses and neurologists, they removed all of the tubes from her arm.

Her prognosis was excellent. She had scored a solid "eight" on the Rancho Los Amigos scale, which measures recovery in brain injured patients. An eight meant her responses were "purposeful-appropriate," that she was alert, conscious of who she was and where she was, as well as able to recall past and recent events—well, most of them anyway. In twenty-four hours, if no complications arose, she would be released.

In the early afternoon, soon after they'd moved her to her new room and given her lunch, Detective Cruz came to speak with her. Lacey shook her head in apology and told the detective she recalled almost nothing about the day she'd been attacked.

"I remember sitting at the breakfast table in my friend Adele Levenson's kitchen. And drinking orange juice. Adele agreed to watch my baby while I went downtown to see my friend, Barnaby Cole, at his loft. I know I went there. I know I was mugged there, because I've heard everyone talking about it. But actually *remember* it? I'm sorry. I don't."

Detective Cruz reassured her that her attacker was in custody. And a pipe wrench had been discovered in the alley behind her friend's building. The wrench had bits of Lacey's blood and hair on it and also a very clear thumbprint matching that of the man they had apprehended in possession of her shoulder bag.

"I think he'll be going away for quite a while," the detective predicted.

"I have only one question for you, Detective."

"Hit me with it, Mrs. Severance."

"When can I get my purse back?"

"I suppose we don't need to hold it much longer, since we're no longer dealing with the possibility of a homicide."

"You mean I'm going to live?"

"It would appear so," the detective said dryly. She gave Lacey a card. "Drop by the precinct when they let you out of here. You can pick it up then—or have your husband do it today, if you'd like. And be sure to give me a call if anything else about the incident comes back to you."

Lacey promised that she would.

Not long after the detective left, the nurse brought Rosie in for a feeding. A few minutes later, Jenna and Mack arrived with Ian. Lacey got to take her nephew in her arms for the first time, while Jenna held Rosie. The sisters agreed that their children were the best, the most attractive and the brightest in the world.

"I can't believe you're really here." Lacey held out her hand and Jenna took it. "It's almost worth getting beat on the head with a pipe wrench, just to look at your face and hold this little boy."

"Hey," Mack complained teasingly, "what about me?"

"You know I'm *always* grateful to see you," Lacey told him.

"We'll stay for as long as you need us," Jenna vowed.

"Watch what you promise me. I may never let you go."

As the sisters admired their babies, Adele and Barnaby appeared. Adele carried a huge bunch of daisies in a big crystal vase. "These are from Xavier and Sophia."

Barnaby presented an arrangement of yellow daylilies. "Belinda Goldstone sent these."

Lacey beamed at the flowers. "Daylilies. They're beautiful. And Xavier knows how I love daisies. Put them all on that ledge up there by the TV, where I can see them."

The flowers were duly set on the ledge. There was no space anywhere else. The room had begun to look like a florist shop. Jenna, Adele and Barnaby had each brought in their own offerings earlier. About an hour before, a lovely creation of birds of paradise and antheriums had arrived from Dan and Fiona. And a bouquet of white roses had come from the Wyoming Bravos.

For a few minutes, Jenna and Mack and Adele and Barnaby all gathered around Lacey's bed. They talked in hushed, happy tones of how good it was to be here, with Lacey awake now, on the road to full recovery.

Too soon, Jenna handed Rosie to Adele. She turned back to Lacey. "Better give me that baby and get some rest."

Lacey rubbed her nose against her nephew's sweet wrinkled neck. "I just don't want to let him go…"

"Come on."

"Oh, all right." She passed the warm bundle into her sister's arms and lay back with a sigh, smiling drowsily, thinking that the lump on the back of her head could still ache like the devil and wondering where her husband had wandered off to. From that first time she woke up yesterday, he had been there whenever she opened her eyes—attentive and so gentle. And a little bit… what? Subdued, maybe. Or even sad.

They needed to talk. They just hadn't had the chance.

And where was he now?

"Where's Logan?" she asked. "I haven't seen him since they wheeled me out of ICU."

"I believe he mentioned some errand he had to run," Jenna said. She sounded just a little too mysterious.

"All right." Lacey looked from her sister, to her brother-in-law, to her friends. "What's up?"

Mack advised, "Take a nap, Lace. He'll be here when you wake up."

One by one, they all tiptoed out. Lacey was asleep before the door shut behind them.

Sometime later, Lacey heard whispering. Very familiar whispering.

She opened one eye and then the other. And then she blinked. "Mira? Maud?"

Giggling in delight, one on one side of the bed and one on the other, the twins grabbed her in a three-way hug.

Lacey hugged back as hard as she could. "Oh, I can't believe it. Tell me I'm not dreaming…"

"You're not dreaming," Maud promised, hugging tighter.

"How did you get here?"

"Logan sent for us," Mira declared.

"Got us plane tickets," added Maud.

Mira pulled away and winked. "First class, doncha know."

The dimples on either side of Maud's mouth twinkled merrily. "The only way to go…"

Mira giggled some more, kissed Lacey wetly on the cheek, and then dropped with a grunt to the chair next to the bed. "I sang for him, on the ride here from the airport. 'When a Man Loves a Woman.' He was duly impressed."

"You bet he was," agreed Maud. "He says he's bringing you to hear us play, the first Friday you guys get back home."

Mira said, "The man is transformed. It's a miracle. What did you *do* to him?"

Lacey lay back on her pillow and grinned. "If I told you, I'd have to kill you."

The sisters groaned in unison, then demanded to know everything that had happened since Lacey came to L.A. Lacey obliged them, filling them in on all the details of her visit with Adele and her meetings with Belinda. She told what she knew of the attack that had landed her at Twin Palms Hospital.

"But you're coming home soon," Mira said hopefully, once the story was told.

"In the next few days, I think."

The twins fell on her for more hugs. Lacey surrendered to their lavish affection. They stayed for an hour. But then they decided they were hungry. Logan had given them a rental car. They wanted to check out L.A. a little and get a sandwich—or maybe two. And they'd be back around again to see how she was doing in a few hours.

They strutted to the door, pausing long enough to blow her more kisses, and then they were gone.

A nurse poked her head in and asked if Lacey needed a Tylenol. "No, thanks. I'm okay."

She closed her eyes and settled back, a contented smile curving her lips.

She didn't even hear him enter.

But she knew he was there when his lips brushed hers.

With her eyes closed and her mouth still pressed to his, she lifted her arms to encircle his neck. "Umm…"

He deepened the kiss, but not too much, his tongue entering just enough to caress the moistness beyond her parted lips. Then he pulled back. She let him go with reluctance, sighing a little, her eyelids fluttering open.

"Oh, look at you. You shaved."

"And showered, too. I needed it," he said gruffly.

"Any way you come to me, you are a sight for sore eyes."

He kissed the tip of her nose, then pulled back again. "I have something to say."

She looked at him sideways. "This sounds ominous."

"It's not. It's…damn hard, that's all. For a man like me."

"A man like you?"

He nodded—and lightly ran his index finger down the curve of her cheek. "An arrogant man. A proud man. A man who always knows he's in the right."

"Surely you're speaking of someone else."

"No, I'm not. And you know I'm not. Lacey, I—"

She reached up once more, this time to put her fingers to his lips. "Oh, Logan. I know."

He caught her hand, kissed it, then folded their fingers together. "Your sister told me you knew. But you do want to hear it." A hint of a smile came and went on that wonderful mouth of his. "Don't you?"

She couldn't seem to keep from sighing. "Yes. It's true. The words do mean something. They mean…a lot."

He said it, very slowly, with just the right blend of tenderness and passion. "I love you, Lacey Severance. I love you with all of my heart. I…thought I knew it all. I thought I knew how to love. I believed that I loved your sister. Because I had decided she was the right woman

for me. But I didn't even know what it was, to love. I...
hell. Maybe I just never learned."

She thought of his cold, distant father. Of the mother
he had never known.

He said, "I don't know how long I've loved you. I
don't think it matters. Maybe forever. Maybe I've been
fighting it for years. But when I finally had you, when
you married me and were my wife, I...didn't want to
admit to myself how important you had become. And
more than that, most of all, I didn't want to lose you.
I've been so afraid of losing you...

"Sometimes it seems to me that I was never really
alive, until that day in September when you first came
to me. And during those months after you broke it off,
I was so damn miserable. You can't know what it felt
like when I got your letter about the baby. And I knew
I would *have* to marry you. That what I wanted with
every beat of my heart was also my duty. God, I was
happy. I was in heaven."

"But you—"

He kissed her hand again. "Let me say the rest.
Please."

She nodded. "Yes. All right."

"I saw your painting as a threat, to me, to what we
had together. And the twins—they scared me, too.
Anything you loved and wanted, anything you cared
passionately for that wasn't me or Rosie. Those things
seemed to only be ways I could lose you. And visiting
Jenna, the idea of that scared the hell out of me. I knew
that as soon as I saw your sister's face again, the truth
would no longer be something I could avoid. I would

recognize her for what she is. My longtime friend. And my wife's sister. And that's all."

"Oh, Logan. I just… I want to kiss you."

"Wait. In a minute. I have to finish this. To say that I never told you I loved you because I felt a little less scared of what losing you could do to me, as long as I thought you didn't know. As long as I kept it from you, as long as I didn't give you that power. And I hate myself, for not coming to you the other day after we talked on the phone and you asked me for the last time. If I had come, you wouldn't have been alone when you went downtown, you wouldn't have—"

"Stop. Stop. Enough."

"Lacey—"

She shook her head. "No. It is not your fault that some desperate fool whacked me on the back of the head. You can't have the blame for that. Do you understand?"

Slowly, he nodded. "All right."

"Good."

She watched his Adam's apple bob up and down as he swallowed. And she thought of that afternoon at the end of June, when he'd come to Wyoming to find her and she'd watched him swallow the ginger ale she gave him and wanted to press her mouth against his throat.

"Bend down to me," she commanded, reaching for him again, hooking her arm around his neck.

He came close, and she kissed him, a deep, sucking kiss on his strong, tanned throat.

When she let him go, he rubbed the spot. "That's going to leave a mark."

"I know."

"I don't believe you did that."

"Believe it."

"I love you, Lacey Severance."

"I know. You said that."

"I'll say it a hundred times."

"You'll say it a thousand, a thousand times a thousand. And so will I. We'll say it to each other every day. Morning, noon and night. Until we're old and tired, and…and *still* we'll say it. Until they lay us in the grave. Oh, Logan, please believe me. We're going to have a wonderful life together."

"Swear it."

"I swear it. Now, bend down again. We'll seal it with a kiss."

He bent close. Their lips met.

Logan closed his eyes.

Even the darkness behind his lids seemed to pulse with color. He smiled against his wife's soft mouth, at last fully understanding exactly what he'd found with her.

Love.

The end of loneliness.

And the beginning of his very own happily ever after.

* * * * *

FAMOUS FAMILIES

YES! Please send me the *Famous Families* collection featuring the Fortunes, the Bravos, the McCabes and the Cavanaughs. This collection will begin with 3 FREE BOOKS and 2 FREE GIFTS in my very first shipment— and more valuable free gifts will follow! My books will arrive in 8 monthly shipments until I have the entire 51-book *Famous Families* collection. I will receive 2-3 free books in each shipment and I will pay just $4.49 U.S./$5.39 CDN for each of the other 4 books in each shipment, plus $2.99 for shipping and handling.* If I decide to keep the entire collection, I'll only have paid for 32 books because 19 books are free. I understand that accepting the 3 free books and gifts places me under no obligation to buy anything. I can always return a shipment and cancel at any time. My free books and gifts are mine to keep no matter what I decide.

268 HCN 9971   468 HCN 9971

Name	(PLEASE PRINT)	
Address		Apt. #
City	State/Prov.	Zip/Postal Code

Signature (if under 18, a parent or guardian must sign)

Mail to the **Reader Service**:
IN U.S.A.: P.O. Box 1867, Buffalo, NY 14240-1867
IN CANADA: P.O. Box 609, Fort Erie, Ontario L2A 5X3

* Terms and prices subject to change without notice. Prices do not include applicable taxes. Sales tax applicable in N.Y. Canadian residents will be charged applicable taxes. This offer is limited to one order per household. All orders subject to approval. Credit or debit balances in a customer's account(s) may be offset by any other outstanding balance owed by or to the customer. Please allow 4 to 6 weeks for delivery. Offer available while quantities last. Offer not available to Quebec residents.